Stubborn Spirits

Fascinating stories of Ohio Ghosts

Rita Arnold

White Dog Books

ISB # 978-09842351-3-1
Library of Congress Catalogue

Cover design by Ron D'Allessandris

Photo on back cover by Michael H. Arnold

Printed in the United States of America

Author's Notes

This is for everyone who enjoys a good ghost story.

Many of the locations and the names have been changed to protect the people involved. If you think you know these locations and the people, please respect their desire for privacy.

Read and enjoy the stories.

This book was written with love,
And of course with lots of care,
The stories that are told within,
Are events that only ghosts would dare!

-   Milton H. Arnold

Other books by Rita Arnold

Ghosts of Darke County
Ghosts of Darke County II
Ghosts of Darke County III
Ghosts of Darke County IV
The Ghosts Among Us
The Ghosts of Western Ohio

Table of Contents

Rita Arnold

1. The Campground Story

In Western Darke County lies an isolated, large, densely wooded area, which was developed years ago for camping with room for about fifty campers. The land rolls like old fashioned Christmas ribbon candy. The trees are large and stately providing plenty of shade for the narrow dirt roadways twisting throughout the campgrounds. The roads meander, giving each camping spot an isolated feeling. A creek with a good supply of fish runs along the eastern boundary. This campground has been in existence since the early 1920's when many Americans first tried family camping vacations and weekend get-a-ways.

Two men were the year round full time maintenance staff with additional summer help for grass cutting and other handyman jobs required around the campgrounds. Bill was the senior employee with twenty five years at the facility. The newest man was Zack who was just completing his first year of work.

1

Stubborn Spirits

Bill and Zack worked well together and enjoyed each other's company. The original wood storage barn remained across the road from the campgrounds. The field around the barn was always mowed and well cared for, but the men rarely entered the old building. Kids played in the open field and during big weekend events, the ground was used for overflow parking. People near the old structure would stop what they were doing and just stare at the barn. Were they seeing something or hearing something?

One day while Bill and Zack were eating lunch in the shade of the old maple tree, Zack looked across the street and asked Bill,

"Do you ever have a strange feeling when you walk by that old barn?" Bill was quiet for a few minutes, and then he looked at Zack and decided to tell him the following story.

~

This was the post World War II era and many people were enjoying tent camping or using small campers shaped much like a tear drop. People wanted to get out, see the country and visit with folks. The war was over and food and gas rationing was no longer in effect. Television, video games, and computers were not camping equipment during that era. Playing sports, fishing, hiking, dancing in the evening to live music, and socializing were the popular activities.

Across the road from the main campgrounds were baseball diamonds, volleyball courts, and a large covered picnic shelter used for live country music on the weekends. A big old wooden storage building was just beyond the baseball field. This was used for storing the lawn mowers, sports equipment and cleaning supplies. It also housed the office for the maintenance manager and a lounge for the campgrounds employees. Sadly, now all that is left are remnants of the baseball field over grown with weeds and the weather worn wooden storage barn. This part of the camping facility is seldom in use today.

The campground ownership has been in the same family since its very beginning. The owners are proud of the fact that they run a clean and well organized facility. They always pick up the litter. The large shade trees and thick bushy shrubs are trimmed and beautiful annual flowers are planted each spring to supplement the perennials that bloom all summer. The only changes over the years have been the upgrading of the grounds for the accommodating of modern campers using the newer large RVs. Today's sparse tent camping is done by the kids of RV parents who supervise from nearby for a night or two.

From December 1st until April 15th the campground is closed. Some people pay to park their campers there the year round but there is no actual camping during these winter months. This is the time of year when the maintenance workers fill in potholes in the roadways, trim or plant any new landscaping items and other necessary maintenance.

During the winter months the weather can suddenly become stormy with blizzard like conditions making travel nearly impossible. Sometimes when Mother Nature makes it too dangerous for the maintenance workers to drive home, they spend the night on cots in the storage barn lounge. This does not happen very often; in fact, over the years only three or four times have the workers been forced to spend the night due to the inclement weather. Of course, it only took one dark, stormy winter night years ago for a good story to develop.

In the late 1950's a sudden blizzard roared in from the Northwest late on a Friday afternoon. The men were repairing an engine in the maintenance barn and did not have a radio with them. Therefore, they had no idea just how icy the drifting snow had become. Portable radios were owned by only a few people, and besides, radio reception was not good in the barn. In addition, being in a rural location, it was common for the telephone to go dead during any type of bad storm.

When the two workers were finished for the day and ready to head for their cars they were greeted by a white surprise when they opened the barn door. The snow was up to their knee caps and was a mixture of snow, ice, and sleet. The wind was howling and blowing so hard that the men could hardly breathe until they shut the door and remained inside. They leaned against the door and stood soundless, astounded by what they just saw.

For a few minutes the two men just looked at each other in stunned silence! They decided that there was no way they could drive home that night, especially since they both lived on distant farms and needed to drive over unplowed snaking, narrow country roadways. Ted, a young fellow who lived by himself, had no reason to call anyone about not coming home that night, quickly decided to stay in the barn. He knew that his livestock would be okay until morning. Otto, who was a few years older than Ted, went to telephone his wife about staying at the campgrounds but was not surprised to find the phone lines were out of order. The men knew that it would be a long and chilly night in the barn but there was no other choice.

Both of them were lucky because the barn was very well built in the post and beam fashion with a lounge area that was well insulated and contained a small, wood potbelly stove. There was some coffee, cookies, crackers, and a small container of vanilla ice cream in the old refrigerator. All in all, the situation was not too bad. Then about an hour later they lost power and all the lights suddenly went out. Otto was able to find a flashlight after rummaging in a tool chest and that was their only source of light.

Using some extra jackets and a couple of old dirty tarps that were used to cover the stored equipment the men fashioned temporary bedding for the night. As the wind continued to blow the fellows lay down and drifted in and out of sleep. A couple of hours later, they were awakened by sounds coming from the east wall.

Step....drag....step....drag....

The howling wind pushed the snow into higher and higher drifts. They decided that it was just too dangerous to investigate the strange noise.

"Probably just the wind blowing debris against the building," Otto suggested.

"Or some poor animal," Ted added. The men nervously went back to bed and again tried to sleep only to be awakened a few minutes later by:

Step....drag....step....drag..........

This time the noise was on the south side on the building and getting louder.

"I'm goin' outside. Someone might be in trouble and need our help," Ted said.

"Don't do anything stupid," Otto replied. "You could get severe frostbite or freeze to death."

Otto lay back down to sleep while Ted sat in a chair, too wide awake to sleep, not admitting that he was scared about the cause of the noise. Ted soon began to pace around and around the large work room too agitated to rest. Then in the silence save for his footsteps, from the south wall he heard:

Step.....drag.....step.....drag............

Ted, visibly shaking, quickly put on his coat, grabbed the flashlight and ran outside to look for the cause of the noise.

"Ted, Don't!" Otto called to his receding back.

Because Ted had taken the only flashlight, Otto put on his jacket to stay warm and waited in the dark just inside the barn door, listening for Ted's return. The comfort of the flashlight made Otto feel warm but the total lack of light in the barn was causing him to shiver – or was he worried about Ted's welfare? Otto kept telling himself that he was over-reacting.

Several minutes went by but Ted did not return. Then an hour passed and still no Ted. Otto paced back and before the double barn door listening for Ted. Time seemed to stand still and Otto feared the worse for his friend. Was Ted lost in the snow storm? Was he injured? What was going on outside? Otto wanted to head outside and search for Ted but he was afraid that he would suffer some horrible consequence. Otto kept thinking about the family whom he loved dearly and were waiting for him at home. He did not want to leave them. Then along the west wall Otto heard:

Step......drag......step......drag..........

Now Otto had a serious decision to make. With at least four hours till dawn, no flashlight, the wind blowing like mad, snow now drifting up to his waist – what should he do? Should he risk his life looking for his friend and possibly die in the process? Should he wait for daylight and pray for the best? Then he heard:

Step.........drag...........step...........drag...........

Suddenly, a heavy weight hit the old wooden double doors in the front of the barn. Otto knew that the long wooden bar was securely in the brackets but would not hold the doors shut much longer with strong hits like that. With another loud crash against the doors, making the distinct sound of wood splintering, Otto knew that the doors would soon break down. Turning quickly on his heels, he headed stumbling, tripping over objects on the floor for the lounge falling in the dark over a lawn mower. He managed to grab a large crow bar as he stood up and headed once again for the lounge.

Otto tried to be as quiet as possible once he was safely in the lounge. He shut the door and stood leaning against the wall. Soon his chest started to hurt because he was nervously holding his breath, too afraid to breathe. His heart was hammering so hard and loudly that he could scarcely hear, and his ears began to pound. Shortly Otto could not stand still and began to shuffle his feet, hopping from foot to foot.

Then he heard a loud crash as the double doors suddenly burst open with the sound of wood splintering and boards breaking. The wind was howling as if an airplane were coming through the double doors. The snow was swirling every where with debris flying and crashing all about! Then he heard heading straight for the lounge:

Step.......drag.........step........drag...............

Raising the large crowbar high over his head and gripping it with both hands that were shaking, big burly Otto stood beside the closed lounge door and waited and waited. The sound came closer and closer and then, suddenly it stopped. After a few seconds of silence, very softly he heard "Ottooooooo, Ottooooooooo." Then, deafening silence. Then the soft sound of a hissing could be heard just outside the lounge door.

After a short time, which to Otto seemed like hours, he could not stand the silence any longer and carefully, very carefully, opened the lounge door and peeked out into the work room. Not sure of what he saw, he threw open the door ready to strike at whatever was on the other side of it. Otto found himself looking directly at Ted who was helping another man and was pulling a new red Radio Flyer wagon with a box of groceries sitting inside the wagon.

After everyone was able to calm down, the men went into the lounge to wait for daybreak. The stranger told them he was driving home from town with the new wagon for his young son when the storm hit. He knew the barn was nearby but because of the wind and blowing, drifting snow he had difficulty finding the barn door. The wagon was a Christmas gift he'd bought in town for his boy and was the only present he could afford. The groceries were desperately needed at home and he could not leave them out in the storm.

When daylight broke, the man and his wagon were gone. Ted and Otto were finally able to hike to a neighboring farm for better shelter and food. The men told the story of the night in the barn with Otto telling everyone that he was never afraid and knew all along the cause of the noise. Ted, who always admired Otto as a father figure, never contradicted his account of that night. The men continued to work together at the campgrounds for several years. They only spoke about that night during the winter season and then only when they were by themselves.

The old barn still stands. Due to age and a deteriorating condition the barn leans to one side. Bats, snakes, and other wildlife now call this old barn home. A few old forgotten tools are scattered across the dirt floor.

It is not safe to use this old building but no one wants to tear down the structure. A newer large, metal building was constructed on the camping side of the road to be closer to the actual campgrounds. The owners say this was for the convenience of the workers. But some people think it was because the maintenance workers claim that on a winter, stormy night the power will fail, the telephones will die, and you will hear:

Step........drag......step.....drag......

Stubborn Spirits

2.   The Bridge

I *spoke to a large group in Shelby County a couple of years ago, telling my ghosts stories and listening to their stories in return. After the meeting concluded, one older, soft spoken gentleman shyly walked towards me and asked for a few minutes of my time. He'd grown up in Ashtabula County in the 1940's and 1950's but now lived in Shelby County. The following is his story.*

In the late 1860's train travel in Ohio was increasing at a rapid pace. The Civil War was over and the industrial North was growing and producing more goods then ever before. Since the mid western part of the country saw only sporadic battles and did not suffer any major destruction of property during the war, growth quickly began in manufacturing and transportation.   Few   roads   or   railways   needed   repair; therefore, travel soon increased at a rapid rate. The North was laying new train tracks, adding additional lines and building bridges for rail traffic to transport goods and people. Some of the new rail lines went from the east coast across northern Ohio to Chicago and on to other western cities.

During the late 1860's Mr. Charles Collins, a district supervisor for the railroad was asked by the railroad company to construct a new bridge over one of the many rivers in the northern part of Ohio. Charles looked at many designs, developed some new ideas of his own, considered some of the old proven designs, and reviewed a few variations on the old and new plans.

Several years later, in 1875, Charles was under pressure to finally choose a design and get the bridge built quickly. The company had waited over ten years for his decision and demanded that the much needed bridge be built immediately. Due to great pressure from Charles' boss, a design was finally chosen but not by Charles. Charles worried that the plans were not structurally sound but he had no choice; his supervisor had mandated the use of this particular design.

A few years later, Charles discovered that the bridge designer was his boss's nephew. He was very well paid for the modern plan even though it was the young man's first bridge design for railroad use. An interesting fact was that this was the nephew's first bridge design used by the railroad company. In fact, this was to be the first bridge design to be constructed for transportation use by a company!

The bridge was completed in almost record time and the tracks were laid. Charles was still concerned about the design and safety of the bridge. Especially due to the speed of the bridge construction Charles raised some doubts about the quality of the workmanship and the materials that were used.

Whenever Charles mentioned his fears to his supervisor, the boss berated him for jealously over a better, more contemporary design. "Just get the job done and quite complaining," was heard so often that Charles finally did just that. The bridge finally became operational in the fall of 1875.

The company was pleased that train travel was, at last, flowing nicely along the new northern route. This made train travel to North Ohio and other western destinations much quicker and more comfortable for the public. Remember, the only other methods of transportation were wagon or horse back during that era.

In late December of 1876 the winter weather suddenly took a turn for the worse. A blinding snow storm quickly moved through the area and soon developed into a blizzard. The wind was fiercely blowing in from Lake Erie bringing a combination of snow and ice, making limiting visibility to only a few miles. The rails were soon slick with ice.

The passenger train cars during those years were constructed mainly of wood and each car had a small coal burning stove to provide some heat for the travelers. Along the walls of each car were sconces that held candles giving off a small amount of golden light.

Near midnight, with the storm growing worse every minute, the small train, composed of less than twenty cars, slowly approached the bridge. The engineer's main thoughts were to get the passengers safely to the depot which was just west of the new bridge and there the passengers could wait out the storm.

Despite the engineer's many years of experience running a train he suddenly grew extremely nervous. This was a new emotion for him. Not since his first run over twenty years before had he felt such a strong case of anxiety. What was happening to him?

The train started slowly across the bridge when suddenly, as the engine approached the other side of the river, the engineer felt a sudden lurch as the back of the engine car gave way and started falling backward toward the water. Quickly he opened the engine to full throttle hoping to get the complete train to the other side of the bridge before a disaster could happen.

Unfortunately, the engine broke loose from the train and only the locomotive made it safely to the other side of the bridge. As the brakes were quickly applied, the engineer looked back at the passenger cars and watched in shocked horror as the rest of the train plunged into the river more than fifty feet below.

The engineer jumped down from the train and raced back to the edge of the river. Wanting to help the passengers but not sure what to do he stood there in shock, staring at the jumbled, tangled ruin of his train.

When the brakeman finally came to stand beside the engineer, they both stared in stunned silence as the passenger cars burst into a flaming inferno due to the burning candles and the coal stoves. It was several minutes before either man was able to move as they stood frozen with horror at what they were witnessing.

The brakeman ran as quickly as possible in the strong wind and snow to the depot while the engineer headed down to the river hoping to assist any possible survivors. Due to the stormy weather and despite the fact that the depot was only a short distance from the bridge, much time elapsed before the brakeman could reach the depot and summon help and run back to the accident scene to help.

The wood passenger cars quickly became a burning hellhole with smoke and screams and the stench of burning flesh filling the night air. With no fire department in the area, the two men could only watch and pray that the passengers would not suffer. Hours later, when the fire had burned itself out and the wreckage was being cleared, the dead were taken to a nearby cemetery for immediate burial. Some travelers survived the ordeal with only minor injuries, but unfortunately, most either died from the fire, or later died from their wounds. Tragically, a few passengers' remains were never found.

The coroner and railroad investigator ruled a few weeks later that the stoves were not properly installed in the passenger cars because they should have extinguished on impact. But more importantly, they concluded that the bridge's design was such that it was doomed to collapse under the weight of a train. AS such, they ruled that the bridge was not a proper, safe design. The investigators also had doubts about the quality of workmanship but too much of the bridge was destroyed in the disaster for anything to be conclusively proven.

Charles Collins was required to testify at the coroner's hearing. He had been in a state of shock ever since the accident and had not spoken of that tragic night. Charles testified that he never liked the chosen design and had visited the bridge weekly to check on the condition of the structure. After the first few weeks of use, Charles wrote letters to his supervisor recommending repairs. These repairs were not scheduled until the following year much to Charles' dismay.

After his testimony, Charles returned directly home without speaking to anyone or making any stops on the way and went slowly upstairs to his small bedroom. There he sat silently on the side of his bed, just staring at the wall but seeing nothing..

Later that day, still silently reliving the train tragedy, tears began to roll down his face; tears he couldn't stop. Charles knew the accident should never have happened. Hour after awful hour passed, his guilt crushing him like a vise across his chest. Robotically, he took his handgun from the top dresser drawer. He slid one bullet in the chamber, carefully placed the barrel to his head and pulled the trigger.

Charles was buried the next day next to his family in a different section of the same cemetery as the accident victims. His graveside services were attended by his living relatives and a few friends. Nobody blamed Charles for the terrible tragedy; nobody except Charles himself.

The railroad employees felt that the supervisor and his nephew should have been held accountable for the bridge's collapse.

The citizens of Ashtabula erected a monument for the accident victims, placing it in the cemetery. Now, over a hundred years later the monument remains in good condition, with the surrounding grass always mowed and fresh flowers planted yearly around the base. This is done by persons unknown. The important fact is that the monument is cared for.

More than a century later, whenever blizzard conditions occur in late December and the clock nears midnight, people still hear the sound of a train wreck, followed by the crackling of a fire and the horrifying screams of people crying for help.

No one has seen visions of the wreck taking place, but the sounds of a train wreck are unmistakable. Residents have no doubt about what they are hearing. Some actually dial 911 for help, believing an actual train wreck happening near by, but nothing is ever found.

The cemetery is also the site of unusual events. People who live near the graveyard claim to see visions of people walking around dressed in dirty, torn clothing as if they are searching for something or confused about where they are. They are dressed in the style of the late 1800's.

Some people report a strange odor, not realizing it is the stench of burnt flesh but no fire is visible in the area. When this happens, the visitors will leave the area immediately and vow never to return! Others will feel sick to their stomachs and need a few minutes away from the site before feeling normal again..

As for Mr. Collins' gravesite, no sightings or events have ever been reported. But anyone who visits his gravesite comments about the strong feeling of sadness that overcomes them. Several people will begin to cry uncontrollably and promise to never return. Visitors do not want the public to know if a sighting or vision does appear. They want Charles to rest in peace – if possible.

3.   Connie's Father

A co-worker told me about her experience with a ghost that began at her family's farm house a few years ago and continues to this day.

Connie grew up on a farm just north of Troy, Ohio in the 1950's. Like all farm kids she learned the value of a good work ethic early in life. She enjoyed working along side her father in the fields and helping with the livestock. As the youngest of three children, and the only girl, she and her dad, Elmer, were very close. Her mother died of cancer when Connie was very young and her father raised the children on his own. Connie's aunt lived nearby and helped as much as possible but she had her own family to care for.

Her father always encouraged her to further her education by learning a skill that would also provide a good, steady, living. Elmer taught her that farming was a good, satisfying life but unpredictable in providing an income and that a time would come when she would need to find work away from the farm.

So, when Connie graduated from high school in 1965, she left home to attend a nursing school in Dayton, Ohio, where she earned her R.N. degree. Connie never married and soon purchased a house just south of Dayton but often visited her Dad on the farm. She wasn't fond of traveling, so she vacationed with her father at her favorite place in the world, this land was her home and her heart.

She had a brother who lived two miles west of Elmer and an aunt just down the road from him, living on her own farm. Still, Connie enjoyed being with her Dad and helping on the farm. Her brother and father worked together every day on Elmer's thousand acres. Connie's aunt fixed the meals for Elmer several evenings a week, but Elmer enjoyed fixing his own breakfast.

Elmer was born in that farm house just like his brothers and sisters before him. He lived there his entire life with happy memories of a childhood spent with his siblings. For about ten years, Elmer's brother, Homer, lived with him.

They had been close all their lives and living together was good for both men.

Sadly, one summer afternoon Elmer found Homer collapsed in the garden from a sudden heart attack. Connie rushed home as soon as she received the call about her uncle's passing. Homer was the brother to whom Elmer was the closest, and unfortunately, Homer passed away in 1974.

By the late 1970's, Elmer was the only sibling left and often complained about being lonely and missing the old days. Sure, his son lived near by and checked on him daily, and Connie returned home as often as possible, but Elmer still missed his brothers and sisters. He frequently said that the problem with growing old was that your friends and family eventually passed away and you were left all alone. He missed visiting with people his own age and sharing common memories.

Connie did what she could to fill her father's days. When not cleaning the house with her aunt, Connie and her Dad worked together in the garden or out in the fields. They always enjoyed each other's company, sometimes talking the day away or sharing a comfortable silence.

One day in 1982 while at work in a Dayton hospital, Connie's brother called with the news that their father had collapsed while working in the garden. Elmer was rushed to the local hospital and was asking for Connie. Within two hours Connie was at her father's bedside, holding his hand and whispering that she loved him as he took his last breath.

Connie could not believe that her Dad was gone. He was her rock; he had always been there for her and she had only a few final minutes to tell him how much she loved him. The pain and shock of his sudden passing overwhelmed her. Connie slowly walked out of the hospital, crying uncontrollably and speaking to no one.

Connie slowly drove back to the farm house to spend the night. She refused offers to stay with anyone. Connie not only needed the comfort of being home, but she also had a strong feeling that she simply had to be there.

The next few days passed in blurred slow motion. Two days later, Elmer was laid to rest beside his beloved Alice in the local cemetery where Homer and the other siblings were all buried with their own families.

Connie got through these sad days with the help of her family, friends, and her faith. Weeks later, she realized that she drew much of her strength during that week from being on the farm in her childhood home. She felt a comfort in the old building with its squeaky wooden floors, the kitchen drawer that always stuck, and the water pipes that burped and groaned. The memories were a tremendous source of strength, almost like the house itself was hugging her.

For the next few weeks Connie spent every minute she could at the farmhouse to sort through her father's belongings. It was difficult for her but she knew this was what her father would have wanted. One day while sorting through his clothing for anything that could be given to charity, she heard her father.

"Connie, please come home," he said. At first Connie thought she was dreaming but again she heard, "Connie, please come home."

Finally, Connie knew what she had to do. She sold her house in Dayton and moved back to the farm. After all, her

Dad had asked her. And this was where Connie found contentment.

After Connie settled in the old house, she started to think that Elmer was hanging around in the kitchen. Connie was afraid that she was grieving too much for her father and starting to imagine things. She decided that she would work harder and longer in the garden and out in the fields. Maybe this could help to ease her heavy sad heart and keep her mind occupied.

Whenever Connie worked in the kitchen in the early morning hours, she heard footsteps coming down the old creaky wooden stairs and heading towards the kitchen.

"What's for breakfast," her father asked, but no one was there.

Twice she saw him standing in the kitchen doorway but he vanished after a couple of seconds. Thinking that she was still grieving for her Dad she decided not to mention this to anyone. Then one afternoon while working in the garden she felt a hand lightly touch her right shoulder. Connie jumped and looked around but soon realized that she was alone, so she just kept pulling weeds.

The second time she felt the hand touch her shoulder she quickly stood up and slowly turned around. There stood her father looking healthier and happier than he had in years. He had a big smile on his face and a twinkle in his eyes.

"Connie, I'm with Homer and the rest of the family and I couldn't be happier. Don't grieve for me. You've got to get on with living. I know you love the farm like I taught you and that makes me smile. Now, girl, you've got to be happy for me. I miss you and the other kids, but I raised you well and I know you'll all be just fine in the world on your own." With that, he was gone.

Connie instantly felt a wonderful peace and happiness come over her. She never shared what happened in the garden with anyone in her family; it was too private of a moment. When she felt sorry for herself about losing her father all she had to do was remember that afternoon in the garden and how happy her father had been.

To this day she still finds an occasional sign that her Dad is with her. His favorite coffee cup will be found placed on the kitchen counter, his favorite chair on the porch is moved closer to the porch railing where he liked to put his feet up and look out over the land, and sometimes his old worn work gloves will be placed beside the gardening tools as if telling Connie, "Girl, it's time to weed the garden." When Connie sees any of this she just smiles and whispers "I love you, Dad."

Connie still happily lives on the family farm and her brother continues living just down the road. Her aunt Alice has passed away and is buried near Elmer.

4.   The Schoolhouse

Whenever someone approaches me who wants to talk about an abandoned schoolhouse located in the country, my eyes light up and a smile appears on my face as I just know that great ghostly tales are involved.

Built around 1910 and located a few miles north of Sidney, Ohio, was a red brick two story school building. No one remembers the reason that the school was built in this exact location but it must have been for a very good reason, since a small cemetery had to be moved before construction could start. It was one of the earliest cemeteries in the area, so maybe plans to move it were already in the planning stages when the need for a new schoolhouse was noted.

After all the bodies were removed and reburied in a new cemetery a few miles down the road, the workers began to dig the basement for the school. Along the east side of the old cemetery, workers found two forgotten basements where two storage buildings had stood years earlier. The above ground structures were long gone with only the flooring remaining to protect the old basements, over which had grown a carpet of thick brush and creeping wild weeds. The school board decided to dig a new cellar and connect it to the previous rooms for additional storage.

When a doorway was cut into the earlier basements, the workers discovered a chilling surprise. Stacked inside, three high, were wooden caskets covered with spider webs and inches of thick dust! These strong men had no desire to look inside the caskets or even to move them. The connecting basement doors were installed in record time and shut tight while the work continued on the school's new cellar. One of the workers expressed surprise that the old wood showed neither visible rot nor damage. The other workers refused to discuss them at all, so the strange find was never reported.

A couple of years later the school was ready for the students. The community was so impressed with the new building that that the old cemetery faded from memory. But some people do not like to be forgotten.

One night, the last teacher to leave the school building heard faint whispers. Thinking that students had returned and could be up to no good, she inspected the entire building but found no one. The math teacher stayed late a couple weeks later to grade some papers and heard footsteps softly walking in the hallway but found no one there. These incidents happened quite often, but no one was ever seen and the source was never found.

The older basement rooms were never used, so the doors always remained closed and securely locked. The only key was located in the janitor's room. As time went by, most people forgot about these seldom used rooms and their contents. But all that would change.

Eli had been the school janitor for over twenty years. He always wore a ring of twenty five to thirty keys on his left hip that jingled whenever he worked. A veteran of World War I, Eli lived a war injury to his right leg causing him to walk with a slight limp. Eli was a hard worker. He took pride in keeping the school clean and everything running in good working order.

During a very cold winter in the 1940's, Eli's wounded right leg was hurting more than normal. One morning he limped down the stairs to the basement to check the furnace when his right leg suddenly, and without warning, gave out. He tumbled down the steps, breaking his neck in the fall.

A couple of hours later the principal went looking for Eli and found him where he had fallen. Eli lay dead on the cold cement basement floor. His head was lying at an odd angle in a pool of blood with his right leg folded under him. The principal quickly summoned the authorities and sent the students home. Later that day, Eli's body was removed to the local funeral home.

The school soon returned to its normal routine and a new janitor, Edward, was hired. He worked at the school until the 1980's when the school was consolidated with another district. Edward, unlike Eli, always carried the keys in his pocket so as to make as little noise as possible.

In spite of Eli's demise, Edward never complained about going down to check on the furnace, but he never lingered in the basement .He told only his wife that he felt uneasy in the cellar, especially on the steps. The bottom of the stairs was always cold; not breezy, just a cold. A few feet away the temperature was always warmer.

The cement floor at the base of the stairs contained blood stains that Edward scrubbed and scrubbed but was unable to remove. The discoloration always left Edward unnerved. He made sure that he never, ever stepped on the blemished concrete. He always stepped around the spot.

At the beginning of many school days, both students and teachers heard Eli's keys jingling as if he was still walking down the hallway. At other times, people noticed the uneven cadence that a man walking with a limp would produce as he made his way across the marble floor.

Early in the 21st century, the old school was torn down. It had stood empty for a number of years and was beyond repair. The structure was quickly demolished with heavy equipment, the debris hauled to a local dump and the old school's land smoothed over. Crops were never planted there. The site became a grassy area with weeds and saplings.

Lately, people have reported seeing unusual lights moving around that lot when no one is there. And, occasionally, the sound of jingling keys is heard.

No one knows if the caskets were they removed during the demolition or left in the ground. People report a strange feeling if they walk across this patch of land, as if someone is watching and wanting them to leave. Several say that they've felt a hand gently press on their backs as if pushing them along.

Those who pass by at dawn's first light sometimes catch sight of a man in worn work clothes, limping along. He may acknowledge you with a nod, but he always keeps moving, the keys on his hip jingling in time to his syncopated gate. Some people call, "Hi, Eli!" If they watch as he passes, Eli will slowly disappear into the morning mist.

5.   The Strangest Man

Mill + creek = ghost. This is a formula that I have found to be true as I collect ghost stories. When someone wants to tell me about their hometown that was established in the early 1800's and the story is about an old mill situated on a nice flowing stream, I know that the above formula will apply. Here is one of those stories.

A friend of mine swears that Greene County is one of the prettiest counties in western Ohio. The pastoral setting that he describes - the curving roads, thickly wooded areas and meandering streams - sounds very picturesque. Add a variety of wildlife roaming through the countryside and you have a pretty picture that is only enhanced by the presence of ghosts.

Shortly after the Civil War, Mr. Abraham Watson settled in the area northwest of Xenia. Seeing the need, he soon built a large grain mill along the major stream that ran through his adopted town. Abe did as much of the work himself as possible, but willingly hired some strong men to help with the heavy lifting. When the time came to construct the mill office, Abe did all of the interior work alone. He did not want anyone in his office at any time. Most of the room's construction was done in the evenings or on Saturday.

Abe lived alone in a small one room cabin near the south edge of town, an easy walk from the mill. His home was nothing fancy, just the basics for living the quiet life. A one room cabin's only luxury was a covered porch across the entire front for sitting in his favorite rocking chair. He never married; therefore, he gave no thought to enlarging his house. He even had no garden out back which was most unusual.

But Abe was always thinking about business, so he continued to increase the size of his mill. Within a few years, he became one of the wealthiest men in the county. The single women tried to engage him in conversation if they found him in the general store, but he would always politely decline their attention.

Abe attended church, but he always arrived at the last minute and sat in the very last pew. When the pastor gave the benediction, he was the first person to leave. If a lady arrived late for church and happened to sit beside him, he did not smile at her or acknowledge her in any way. He was never even seen eating at the one small restaurant in town.

The simple truth was that Watson did not like people. He was always friendly to his customers and kind to his employees, but except for church he did not want to be around anyone. He never invited neighbors to his cabin for a visit and rarely would say more then hello to people when he was shopping for supplies in town. If someone walked past his cabin, he would nod his head in acknowledgement but never say anything or invite them to visit. He just was not a sociable person.

When he did shop for the few household items he needed, Abe only bought the absolute necessities. He wore the clothes on his small bulky frame until the local seamstress could not patch or mend them any more and then she had to convince him that new pants or a new shirt were required to avoid public embarrassment. Then, he insist upon the cheapest fabric that she carried and strongly complain that she over charged for her labor. When he finally paid for the new clothes, he left the store grumbling about the price and stomped all the way back to his cabin.

Abe donated freely to his church and gave anyone a job to help them out. Still, some people were jealous of his rumored wealth and soon rumors were spread that he had a large amount of gold hidden in his cabin. The gossip possibly started because he was never seen transacting any business at the local bank.

Some people speculated that the riches were buried on his property or hidden somewhere in the cabin or the mill. The talk at the local tavern was that the money was concealed under a trap door in the cabin floor or maybe in the mattress, or possibly buried in the ground outside. How the money's location was marked also provided hours of conversation. If Abe heard the rumors or if a bold speculator asked him about them, he neither acknowledged the person nor gave any indication about the story's validity.

The idea of a large sum of money buried like treasure makes stealing very tempting to people who would rather take from others than work for a living. Unfortunately, these rumors persisted and eventually led to Abe's demise.

Early one weekday morning, one of his neighbors was walking past Abe's cabin to work at the mill when he saw someone lying on the ground a few feet in front of the small porch. On closer examination, the neighbor saw that Abe's head had been chopped off and a huge pool of blood had covered the ground.

The neighbor ran the short distance and stumbled into town, screaming for the sheriff. The sheriff and several towns' people quickly returned to find the headless, bloody, torso on the ground and a discarded, blood-covered hatchet a few feet away. The sheriff swiftly found a tattered blanket and covered the badly beaten body. After several days of careful searching, the authorities gave up. The head was never recovered!

No one knew if Abe had any family, so in 1874 Abe was quickly and quietly laid to rest in the cemetery next to the church with only a few people in attendance. A wooden tombstone purchased by the church marked the plot.

His cabin's interior had been ransacked with Abe's few personal possessions scattered about and shattered to pieces. It was impossible to determine if anything had been stolen from the cabin since none of the citizens had ever been in Abe's home. The cabin remained standing for a number of years under various owners. Sadly, the murderer was never found.

Most of the locals refused to go near the house. Mothers would not allow their children to walk near the cabin for fear that the killer was still lingering in the area. Soon, tales surfaced of seeing a headless man walking around the cabin. Most folks accredited these stories to over active imaginations.

Sometime, children on a dare or the occasional adventurous adult, would tell of being approached by a headless man who was stretched his arms out for help. Not surprisingly, the children quickly turned and ran - never to return. Adults never admitted to running, but told their tales with a nervous laugh.

The years passed and people began to move into this area from the east coast. Newcomers were always thrilled to find a cabin to rent at such a low rate in a nice location. But no family ever stayed more than one week and most moved away from the area and never came back. Why?

The renters packed and left so fast that they never asked for their rent money back or explained why they were leaving. Some even left under the cover of darkness, driving their wagons at a hazardous pace. They never gave an explanation for the hasty move from the cabin. The only thing in common was those seen leaving by any of the town's citizens had a look of horror etched upon their faces. Some of the renters were visibly shaking so badly that they had difficulty hitching the horses to the wagon! If asked what had happened, they refused to talk.

The cabin and grain mill are now long gone; not even the foundations remain. Several people think they know the exact location of the structures because they claim to feel a strange, quiet sensation come over them when they are near where the buildings once stood. They report a feeling of wanting to be alone though they never before craved solitude. People were known to wander off and spend several minutes sitting by themselves, not wanting to speak with their friends.

Occasionally someone told of seeing a vision of a headless man walking along the stream, carrying a head under his right arm. Most people take off running at a fast, awkward pace when they see the headless man and never look at the face. They have no desire to look at it! But the few with nerve enough to try, describe a quiet smile fixed on his lips.

And there is one spot where the ground always has dark red-tinged dirt. Locals claim that even if you dig up the dirt and replace it with ground from a different location, you will return to find the same discolored dirt in the original spot.

Though none of the sightseers has ever been harmed in the vicinity of Abe's old mill, no one has returned for a second visit.

6.   The Old Theaters

A few years ago an older lady told me stories of a couple of theaters in Dayton, Ohio. She had relatives who worked in the two different theaters in that Ohio town and over the years they remembered hearing some interesting stories. The relatives would not admit to witnessing any strange events but they knew all the details about what happened. I do not want to use the names of each theater so they will be called Theater A and Theater B (original don't you think?), nor do I wish to do anything to harm the reputation of these fantastic structures that are so important to the town's history. Are the stories true? No one knows for sure, but they are entertaining and well worth the telling.

Both establishments were built over one hundred years ago. Over the years, thousands attended the live performances. Local and nationally famous professional actors appeared on these stages.   Everything from concerts, dramas, musicals, comedies, and graduation ceremonies were housed in these theaters.

I remember being in each theater only once as a young child and was completely astounded at the size of the buildings and the fancy décor. Of course to a child, a building can seem larger than it actually is and with the passing of the years I am sure that the size of each structure has increased in my mind.

Theater A hosted a huge variety of entertainment: dramas, opera, musicals, comedy, and symphonies. Until late in the twentieth century this theater provided a variety of entertainment for the citizens. The theater employed a number of people; both part time as well as a few full time maintenance and housekeeping staff to keep the theater in pristine condition.

Back in the 1950's most employees did not have fancy titles for their jobs. A custodian was a custodian, a ticket taker was a ticket taker, and a maintenance man was a maintenance man, who, in this case was a long-time employee named John. He was walking across the empty stage one afternoon getting last minute chores completed for a weekend performance. He had worked at this theater for over twenty-five years and knew every inch of the building. He had walked on that stage thousands of times as he went about his duties. Something made today's stage check different.

No one knows exactly what happened, but one minute John was walking across the front of the stage checking the floor lights and the next minute he was lying on the floor of the orchestra pit, having fallen over fifteen feet and landing hard on his right hip. John was racked with pain and could not move. He laid there on the cold, hard floor, unable to comprehend what had just happened, while a co-worker raced to summon help.

As late as the 1950's, when a person in their 60's broke a hip, their outlook for recovery was not always good. John was immediately rushed to a nearby hospital for medical treatment. His co-workers were very worried about him, wondering if he would recover from the surgery. Would he be able to eventually return to work? Would he be the old active John that everyone knew and loved?

Unfortunately, a couple of weeks later he passed away at the hospital. His co-workers were shocked. John was more than a colleague; he was a friend and a confidant.

Soon after John's death, several unexplainable events started to happen around the theater. Footsteps were heard on the empty wooden stage near the orchestra pit with no one in sight. The sound was of heavy work boots, not the sound of soft soled shoes worn by some performers. These footsteps were always heard during an afternoon of preparation for an upcoming performance.

Lights on the music stands in the orchestra pit would flicker near where John fell. The orchestra members thought this was the result of John's fall when he bumped a couple of the music stands as he fell into the pit area.

In the locked maintenance room where the tools were kept, John's co-workers found that during the night, the tools had been moved around and organized for the next work day. They would always say, "Thanks John" as a tribute to the pride he had taken in his job.

John's friends took comfort in these events. They began to feel as if John were still with them.

One morning when the crew walked into the maintenance room, they noticed a light bulb on the workbench beside a worker's tool belt. They knew that the bulbs had been stored in the cabinet across the room on the previous night when they left work for home. One worker ignored the light bulb, grabbed his tool belt and headed upstairs to begin the day. Later as he walked across the stage, he noticed a light bulb was burned out near the location where John had fallen. The worker said softly, "You tried to tell me to bring that bulb with me, didn't you, John?"

From that time on, whenever the maintenance crew found a light bulb beside a tool belt, they knew that a burned out bulb on the stage needed replacement. They always appreciated the help from their invisible colleague.

~

Theater B is another older building with a grand history of fantastic performances. In the early 1920's a traveling troupe arrived in town for a four evening performance of a Shakespearian play.

On the second day of the play, the lead actress had finished dressing and decided to step outside for some fresh air. She loved the fancy costumes and makeup for her role and was always ready long before she was cued for her entrance. Her routine was part of her nightly preparation, so she always splashed on her signature scent of lavender cologne before walking around backstage and encouraging her fellow actors

After her nightly visit with the other performers, she stepped out the back stage door into the alley for a breath of cool air on the pleasant evening. Unfortunately, she never returned to portray her character. The stage door man was standing just inside the door and swore that he never heard a sound from the outside. What happened? Did she go for a walk and get lost? Was she abducted?

The local authorities were quickly notified but she was never located. No evidence was found of her having been in the alley. For years afterward a vision of this actress could be seen in the lady's dressing room. At other times, a faint lavender scent permeated the air, though no one was using that perfume.

Actors who stood outside the stage door before a performance complained of a cold sadness coming over them, causing their quick retreat to the dressing rooms. After a few minutes indoors, calm returned and the evening performance came off without a hitch. Others waiting outside the stage door told of hearing a faint call for help, but the source was never found.

There is another intriguing story about Theater B that concerns not an actor, but a patron of the arts. The woman, a prominent socialite, enjoyed the theater tremendously and attended as many performances she could. Though never married, she enjoyed the company of having many proper escorts to the shows.

At the conclusion of one play, our patron, sitting in a box seat along the right side of the theater, was suddenly and viciously attacked by a jealous former boyfriend. Before anyone could restrain him, he was able to beat and then strangle the woman. She never had a chance despite the heroic efforts of several men who attempted to subdue the attacker. She died on the floor beside her much loved favorite seat. In the theater where she had spent so many enjoyable evenings, she breathed her final breath.

The attacker was immediately arrested and taken to the local jail. Justice was swift back then. After a speedy trial before an emotional jury of Dayton residents, the attacker was hanged within a few blocks of where he'd murdered the lady who so love the theater.

For many years after this incident, men who sat in the lady's favorite box had a hard time enjoying their evening because of an overwhelming feeling of being unwelcome. A few said they felt as if they wanted to hit someone, preceded by a sensation of unexplained anger. As soon as they walked out of the box, they would calm down. But when they returned, so did the strange emotions.

In contrast, no woman reported any unusual feelings or emotions, but their escorts sometimes were stunned by a sharp slap on the face. Some of the wives even noticed a reddened mark on their husbands' cheeks that resembled a handprint.

The mark would linger for several minutes and then slowly fade away.

Many people believed the mark on the men's' faces was proof of the society lady still trying to defend herself. No one ever asked for their money back or voiced any complaints. They felt sorry for her, one man wishing aloud that she'd swung harder.

7. The Lonely Cemetery

No one has more respect for a cemetery than I do. For this reason I'll be very vague about the location of this story. I do not want anyone to visit this sacred spot and vandalize the dead.

In Miami County stands an old isolated cemetery, located on a secluded country road. It is a small cemetery with only around two hundred graves with just under one hundred tombstones remaining. The other tombstones have been missing for so long that no one remembers them. This graveyard has not had a burial in many years.

A densely wooded area with huge, wide spreading trees protects the cemetery on all three sides with over grown shrubs and a few trees lining the front entrance. The trees stand tall and straight like soldiers guarding the dead. Visitors can feel the trees silently scrutinizing them, as if always watching over the cemetery residents. An old fence with vines and intertwining weeds circles the cemetery to protect the graves with only a small entrance gate for a person to walk through.

This graveyard is not visible from the roadway. It sits back a long narrow twisting dirt lane that provides privacy for the inhabitants. It's not an easy drive for a car but a fun walk for a hiker.

The cemetery contains the graves of some of the earliest Miami County settlers. These are the people who came here to farm or maybe to open a store or to be the local town doctor. They are the people who wanted to provide for their families and experience the opportunity of living in a new territory. No one buried here became famous by donating land for a school or establishing a large prosperous business. There are no politicians, lawyers, or any other type of prominent persons; they are your every day 'Joe lunch bucket' working class people.

When a person walks into this cemetery he feels a hush come over him. It could be because many visitors can relate to the hard working folks buried here since no one in this lonely spot was ever considered wealthy. The deceased are what we now call plain, middle class folks.

As you read the tombstones, you will notice that several children are buried here. Most of the adult residents did not live beyond their forties. Only one person lived long enough to reach the ripe old age of fifty-three. In the early 1800's, it was highly unusual to live beyond one's fifties.

The tombstones are legible because most of them are protected from the weather by the trees and shrubs. You feel a strange kind of sadness as you walk around the burial ground and read the markers. Why do these monuments all look so new? They lean in different directions due to the ground settling over the years. Some even look ready to fall over, but every inscription is clearly readable. How unusual.

Because the tall trees grow right up to the cemetery fence line, very little sun light comes through. The grass is sparse and the ground always has a soft, damp feel. Even the air feels cool and damp on a hot summer day. You may need to wear a sweater or jacket even on a sticky, sunny July afternoon.

Stubborn Spirits

One unusual characteristic of this graveyard is a single tree standing in the exact middle of this hallowed ground. Walk from this tree to the fence row and you will find that the distance is equal on all four sides. The old tree has a tremendous spread of branches, providing shade for much of the cemetery. There are no other flowers, shrubs or trees within the grounds, not even any tree seedlings or wild flowers.. Just this one solitary, stately tree stands witness in the middle of the stones.

If you visit in the evening and stand quietly in one spot, you will hear footsteps near the front entrance along with the sound of horses with their harnesses softly jingling. Close your eyes and you can easily visualize the citizens bringing a body for burial in an old wooden wagon pulled by two large work horses. Some people have reported that they can smell the horses near the fence where they were tethered. The soft whinny of the steeds is heard near the front entrance, along with the stomp of a heavy hoof that retreats into the distance.

Others claimed to hear the soft crying of people as they weep for their dead. After a while, the voices and the crying start to fade away as if the mourners are leaving the area. The sounds of their grief recede in the direction of the gates.

On rare occasions, a terrified woman screams in a piercing voice from the rear of the cemetery, calling for help. Suddenly, her shouts stop and there is a deafening silence, too painful to endure. Legend has it that a young lady was savagely raped and murdered here when she came to visit her grandfather's grave. Those who have heard her unanswered plea for help, quickly leave the site for the safety and quiet of their homes. Women are left with an overwhelming sense of hopeless rage, often being reduced to tears of frustration at their inability to alleviate her suffering. Many never return after hearing the screams.

Rita Arnold

8. Old Vacant Hospital Buildings

In Montgomery County, the history of hospitals and health care goes back to the 1800's. As the town and surrounding area became populated, the development of industry soon grew at a rapid pace.

By the late 1800's the area was in need proper healthcare facilities. Some of the hospitals had their beginnings with religious affiliations and of course a few hospitals originated to care for the veterans returning from the Civil War. A large multi- building campus was built for the hospitalization of citizens with mental problems.

Through the years many of these hospitals would either completely demolish a building or totally gut the interior in order to update and modernize the structure to provide more up to date health care to the patients.

In the early 1900's, health care was in a learning phase. Antibiotics had yet to be developed and preventive medicine was unheard of. People only came to a hospital when they were so sick that their family did not feel qualified to care for them. When a person needed some type of surgery, a hospital visit was required. Since there was no insurance back then, most people could not afford healthcare. As such, very few people used the hospitals unless it was a life or death necessity.

To protect the identity of the hospitals in this story they will be referred to as Hospital 1 and Hospital 2.

Hospital 1 was built in the late 1800's and served as a general hospital. The single story brick building stood not far from the center of town. When a severe influenza outbreak attacked the citizenry many people were sent to the hospital more for isolation than for treatment. Local officials believed that this approach could prevent the spread of the disease and help protect the healthy citizens.

The children were separated from the adults in a special ward. Very minimal care was provided for the patients of any age. The patients were fed and left to rest most of the day. Occasionally the patients were encouraged to sit in the sunshine or near an open window for fresh air.

The rooms were large wards with possibly twenty or thirty beds per room. There was just enough space between each bed for a nurse or doctor to stand. Wealthy patients would be awarded a private room with a private nurse. Most of the nursing care was provided by single or widowed women who received on the job training.

Over the years, the hospital remodeled the giant wards into large semi-private rooms. Eventually this section became a medical unit that cared for a variety of patients housed in fifteen rooms on both sides of the hall with a nursing station at one end.

Before the oldest building of Hospital 1 was torn down, many employees on the night shift complained of hearing soft moans and groans coming from rooms that had no patients. When the staff checked into the sounds, nothing could be found. Even the televisions were turned off.

Sporadically the staff would report locked doors suddenly being opened when no one in sight. The nurse with the keys could be away from the unit and yet, the locked door would slowly swing open as if someone were going into the supply room. A few minutes later, when a specific medication was needed from the room it would be found placed on the counter just outside the door as if in anticipation.

The employees were never afraid to work the night shift on this unit because no one was ever harmed. In fact, the staff enjoyed hearing the unusual sounds. They felt as if they were working on a special unit. The employees attributed the events to former staff members.

New employees often needed time to adjust to the noises, and some never did. Not everyone was comfortable with hearing the voices but not finding anyone around.

During a slow weekend on the evening shift, one long-time nursing staff employee was in a room at the end of the hallway preparing for the next admission. When her co-workers noted that she had been gone an extra long time, another nurse went down the hall to investigate.

Thinking the nurse needed help with something she called out, "Hey, Jenny. What's taking you so long."

When she entered the room, she found her friend lying on the floor and screamed for help. The rest of the staff came running but all the heroic efforts could not resuscitate Jenny. She died from what later was discovered to be a massive heart attack.

The staff grieved long and hard for their comrade. They were all offered a transfer to a different area of the hospital but no one wanted to leave. This was their unit and Jenny was a special friend.

To this day on the night shift during a time when the patient census is low, the sound of someone making a bed can be heard in an empty room at the end of the hall. If the intercom is turned on, employees will hear the sounds of wrestling sheets and the side rails clanking into a lower position to accept the next patient. Is Jenny still finishing her duties?

Patients in the room across the hall have even complained during the night about the noisy housekeeping. When the staff investigates they find no one in the room and impossible to explain the sounds. Would their patients be comfortable knowing that they were across the hall from a haunted room?

~

Hospital 2 was built in a separate area of town around the same time as Hospital 1. Hospital 2 had a large number of long term employees who dedicated their lives to working at the facility. For years it was difficult to be hired at Hospital 2 because many employees would stay for 35 or more years.

One such employee never married, so her co-workers were her family. Alice was a dedicated and wonderful nurse. She was one week away from turning 65 and beginning mandatory retirement. She was trying to be happy about retiring and spending time with her hobbies, but she was sad to leave work and the people she loved.

One weekend evening while making a bed in preparation for the empty room's next patient, Alice grabbed her chest, gasped and fell to the floor – dead from a massive stroke.

A few minutes later a co-worker walked into the room to help her ready the room, but found poor Alice lying on the floor her eyes staring at the ceiling and her fists clasped at her chest. Help was quickly summoned, but nothing could be done to save Alice. She died on the unit where she had dedicated so much of her life.

As time passed many people forgot about the nurse passing away at work. But how does the staff explain to patients who call the nursing station on the intercom complaining of someone in the room across the hall making a bed and moving the furniture around? Sometimes a patient actually walked across the hallway to talk with whoever was in the room only to find it empty.

One quite evening, a patient asked if the nurse from the previous evening would be working again, saying how much he enjoyed talking with her. As the patient described the nurse to the aide, she realized the description was an exact match of the nurse who had died a year ago on that very day. The aide softly answered no, the nurse would not be working. She could not bring herself to tell the patient that he had been talking to a ghost. The aide quickly walked down the hall to the staff lounge and cried for several minutes. The aide had worked with Alice for several years and missed her friend terribly.

Stubborn Spirits

The oldest building at Hospital 2 is now used only in the daytime. No one can explain why the elevators will suddenly start to move or contain a lingering smell of perfume after the elevator doors open.

Many employees like to attach a ghost story to the elevators, and others just say that it is an electrical problem due to the old wiring. One person said that the elevators keep working to prove that the old building should not be torn down. But no one can explain the fragrance or the voices that are heard on the empty elevators. Today's employees simply accept that their former colleagues are still performing their duties.

9. The Department Store

*W*arren County is a county that respects and protects its past, yet at the same time embraces the future. Drive through this area and see the beautiful homes, the well kept lawns, and the beautiful landscaping. It is so easy to see the pride of home ownership that the citizens have about their properties. One minute you are surrounded by stores and businesses and the next you are driving through beautiful topography. On the farms, horses are grazing peacefully in the pastures, and the barns and houses sit comfortably back from the road.

A large department store was built in the 1980's on vacant ground in the northern section of the county. One oral history insists that an Indian burial ground was located on the property many years ago. Another legend is that a cemetery once stood on this spot, but the tombstones were all stolen and the cemetery was forgotten. Eventually the farmer who owned the land started planting crops and soon all evidence of a cemetery was erased.

As the area developed and businesses came to the locale, this farm and others were sold to a large chain store. Additional surrounding stores were also planned. The development of the land was met with mixed reactions. Some of the citizens missed the old rural area and some were happy to receive a large sum for their land. They all agreed that this was progress.

The store was completed and soon employees reported for work. The grand opening was successful with a large attendance by the public. For the first few weeks, everything went well for the store and its' satisfied customers. But it wasn't long before unusual events began to happen inside the new structure.

Office workers lay their keys on the desk in the morning, and turned around in their chairs to start their computers. When they turned back, the keys were gone. No one else was in the room. A few minutes later the keys would suddenly reappear on the desk but in a different spot. Some mornings, when employees booted up their computers, they found childish drawings on their screens even though no drawing software had been loaded onto the CPUs.

Occasionally, people using the bathrooms reported seeing a faint vision of a sad lady in the mirror. When they turned to look around the room, there was no one there and the vision in the mirror disappeared. Folks broke speed records washing their hands and leaving the restrooms!

The night stocking crew reported seeing a vision of young girl skipping down the aisles. She did not look at the merchandise, just skipped along as if she were going down an old country road. She wore a dark brown plain dress with high top button shoes in the same style that one saw on TV cowboy movies. No one knew her name or why she was there but they talked as if they enjoyed seeing her. One employee said that he truly became a member of the staff after he finally saw the little girl skipping down the aisle!

No one was able to explain the cold spots that were located in the rear of the store near the offices. They were cold enough that people actually started to shiver so much that they had to put on sweaters or jackets. This was not a cold breeze, just a cold spot! As soon workers moved three feet in any direction, they immediately began to warm up.

The employees always seemed to enjoy these events. In fact, new hires were told that they were not officially part of the team until they saw the lady in the mirror or the young girl skipping down the aisle. Most greeted the little girl as she hopped down the aisle and smiled at the lady in the mirror. If a drawing appeared on the computer monitor, the workers would actually say, "Thank you" aloud.

It was a sad day for the employees when the store closed. They felt as if they were leaving behind some good friends. In fact, several employees wrote good bye notes and left them on the office desks and in the restrooms. One young man even left a note on the floor of the aisle where the girl was so often seen happily skipping along.

The building is still vacant – maybe.

10.   The Physician's Office

In the early 1800's many small town country doctors would keep a patient with a serious injury or illness in their office over night to prevent further complications. This was true for the town doctor in a northwestern section of Greene County, Ohio.

Farm families often sent for the doctor to treat the sick person in his own home, where he or she would also recover. During those years there were not many hospitals or physicians who had access to them. Small rural towns were too far away and, with no healthcare insurance, most people could not afford the cost of a hospital stay anyway.

Doctors in the 1800's treated broken bones, sewed lacerations, performed surgery, and pulled teeth, all in their office with minimal medications and few instruments. They learned how to treat all the needs of the people with little education but lots of on the job experience.

Stubborn Spirits

The physician's office was usually located on the edge of town with a small wooden sign posted by the front door. The doctor and his family lived in a wood framed house with the front one or two rooms set aside for the doctor's treatment rooms. Living where you worked was convenient for the doc and the citizens always knew where to find him. It was also economical as most small town physicians could not afford two separate buildings.

In the 1800's, doctors were often paid in goods (firewood, livestock, etc.). It was common for people to have no cash money for some length of time; therefore, the citizens often used the barter system for payment.

Dr. Adams' office was organized in this fashion. Situated on the western edge of town, there was plenty of room for a large garden where he grew herbs and vegetables. He ground the herbs in a mortar and pestle for use as medication, much like the Native Americans did for generations before him. The vegetables helped to feed his family.

Behind the doctor's house was a large barn with room for his horses and the buggy that he needed to visit sick people outside of town. Doc Adams had a nice homestead, especially for a town physician.

Few small towns had an apothecary or pharmacy. Some general stores sold "cure all" type medicines that a traveling salesman convinced the shop keeper to carry. Most remedies were nothing more than flavored liquid containing eighty percent alcohol. Therefore, the town's citizens asked the doctor for some type of pain relief whenever the pain became unbearable.

Dr. Adams had a great reputation for giving good medical care and charging fair prices. If he knew that the family could not afford to pay him, the fee was never mentioned. He would settle for a home cooked meal or maybe some canned goods. Or a few days later he would find a sack of potatoes or baked goods outside his back door. At times, a calf or sheep would be tied to a tree.

He came to the Greene County area shortly before the Civil War to start his practice. Being a bachelor, his younger sister, Sara, lived with him.

Doc Adams was a soft spoken man who rarely raised his voice. He was so skinny that clothes just seemed to hang on his nearly six foot frame. He never wore a western hat, preferring a black derby. His mannerisms made people comfortable and confident in his ability as a physician, but he was still considered to be an ordinary person.

The citizens loved Dr. Adams and the fact that he had a physical handicap never seemed to hamper his ability to provide excellent medical care. His right leg had underdeveloped muscles and was a couple of inches shorter than the left. This made getting around town a little slower for Doc Adams but he managed and never complained.

A few years after moving to the area his sister fell in love and married the man of her dreams. They lived nearby so she continued to care for her brother's house. Daily, she fixed the noontime dinner, did some light cleaning, and took home any clothes that needed cleaning or mending.

One sunny day she walked over to Doc Adams' house carrying a basket on her arm with his meal. After entering the front door, she called out a greeting of hello to be sure the doc was in and not out seeing a patient. Receiving no answer, she headed toward the small kitchen area in the back where Doc liked to eat by the window.

She put the breakfast dishes away, and started to tidy up the kitchen area in preparation for the afternoon meal. Doc usually had books and papers on the table where he liked to read in the evening and these she carefully stacked on the corner of the table. She then grabbed the bucket and headed to the door to get water from the pump and some firewood for the stove.

She opened the back door and let out a loud blood-curdling scream that brought the town's people running to the house. The bucket fell to the ground as she continued to scream with her hands over her mouth and her eyes wide in horror. There, lying on the ground was Doc Adams; his head smashed open and dark red blood pooled all around him. His coat pockets were turned inside out.

The sheriff quickly organized a search party. The area surrounding the house yielded no footprints or blunt objects covered in blood. The posse covered that section of town but nothing of significance was located. Nothing was missing from the house or the barn.

Doc was never known to have more than a few cents in his pockets and he was always willing to share his money. Why Doc was murdered in so brutal a manner made no sense to anyone.

Doc was buried the next day with a short dignified service in the town's cemetery, a wooden marker bearing just his name and the year. It seemed everyone in the area turned out for the funeral. Everyone was stunned and most could hardly talk. The women wept and the men stood in stood silence for several minutes after the funeral.

People started to lock their houses at night. For several weeks they feared that a crazy man was running loose in the area. Mothers refused to allow their children to play outside unless in the company of several other children or an adult.

Doc's sister was so upset that she could not bring herself to clean out the house and office. The building was soon boarded up and everything left just as if Doc was out on a house call and would return later.

Doc's faithful horse was taken to his sister's farm to live out his days. The horse was allowed to run free in the pasture where people noticed that he spent most of his time staring in the direction of Doc's house. A week later the horse was found dead in the pasture with his head looking toward his master's old home. No broken bones were found on the horse and some believed that the poor beast died of pure loneliness for his master and companion.

Many years passed before Dr. John Yoder came to town. Finally, this young, energetic man set up his practice in Doc Adam's old office. Within a month he moved the office to the other side of town into an old run down building. Everyone was surprised at the move and the new doctor gave no explanation for it.

He still owned the original building that housed Doc Adams' office and decided to rent it out for income. Some tenants were found but, unfortunately, they only stayed a few weeks and then moved quickly to another location in town. It was not long before this became a pattern with several occupants. Word soon went around town that old Doc Adam's house was haunted!

During daytime hours, it was common to hear footsteps coming in Doc Adam's front door and going into one of the treatment rooms. This was followed by the front door closing with a loud bang.

Throughout the day, coughing was heard as well as drawers being opened and shut. In the evening, the sound of glass jars lightly banging and the gentle sound of grinding in a mortar and pestle were heard in the kitchen. At the night, quiet talking or soft crying came from the front rooms.

The few tenants who stayed in the house talked about strange activity in the kitchen. Chairs would be pushed under the table at night but the next morning Doc's favorite was pulled back as if someone had sat there reading. The oil lamp was also moved during the night from the hallway stand to the middle of the kitchen table.

Behind the house near the back steps where Doc Adams body was discovered was a two foot wide circle of dark red in the dirt. Folks would use a shovel to turn the dirt over in hopes of obscuring the sinister stain. One person even dug up the dirt, took it to the back of the pasture and brought back fresh top soil. The next day the red area had returned near the back steps!

No one would step on that red spot; hey always stepped around it.

Saddest of all were the sounds coming from the barn. The soft, mournful whinny of a horse was often heard. If you've ever heard the sound of a mare when she is first separated from her foal, then you know this sad, sad sound. When the noise was investigated, the barn was found to be empty of all animals. Yet, the heartbreaking, sad whinny continued. Many people would began to cry on hearing this soft sad wail, and could not stop crying until the whinny stopped or the person walked far enough away that they no longer heard the horse crying.

A few years later Dr. Yoder moved to a town further out west and the town was again without medical care. Many years after old Doc Adams passed away, the perfect new tenant was found for the original office/house combination.

The second Dr. Adams was a widower in his late forties. He was happy with the location and the office setup and soon settled into a nice routine. The town had been without a physician for a few years and the citizens were thrilled to have an experienced doctor back in town.

The townspeople chose not to mention the hauntings to their new physician in the hopes that nothing strange would happen and he would stay for many years. A few months after new Doc Adams had been in practice, he was in the general store doing his shopping. While the doctor was talking with the store owner the topic of having a second Doc Adams in town was mentioned.

New Doc Adams talked about his life back east. After he became a widower he dreamt of living in a rural area in Ohio. He had a distant relative who was a physician in Ohio years ago but he was not sure of the exact location. The mail service was not the best in those years and old Doc Adams was not much for letter writing.

New Doc Adams asked about his predecessor and wondered if there was really a family connection. People laughed about how slim the chances of that would be. Soon they parted ways and Doc strolled back to his office with his purchases to attend to his patients.

That night, when he was sleeping in the bedroom he had a dream and he remembered the dream vividly the next morning. A tall, skinny older gentleman appeared in the dream and softly said, "I did not let anyone stay here, I sent them all away. I saved this practice and this house for you. Please stay. I was your father's cousin."

The second Dr. Adams stayed in town for many years with a successful practice. Soon he purchased a horse and traveled about the territory in old Dr. Adams' buggy. The citizens would look at him driving the buggy and exclaim, "Look – Dr. Adams is back!"

11. The Old Legend

Many creeks run through Darke County and in the early 1800's most of them averaged between three feet to several feet deep. Many were deep enough to provide power for various mills. Young people had the joy of building a raft and floating a ways down the creek on a lazy warm Sunday afternoon.

This is a story that I have heard many times but I can not find any historical documentation concerning the events. Not everything that happened in the early 1800's was reported and some events that were reported in the early newspapers were not always accurate.

In the early nineteenth century, settlers were just beginning to come into the territory though the Treaty of Greene Ville had been signed about twenty years earlier. As development began, the area was mostly wooded with a large amount of swamp land. When the land was cleared, the settlers found excellent soil for growing crops and good pasture land for the livestock.

Children were the same in those days as they are today. They attended school when possible, helped on the family farms, and managed to find some time to play. History books describe children fishing in the creeks to catch for meat that could be enjoyed at the evening meal. But mostly, they just liked to play by the creeks, skipping rocks over the water or swimming on a warm day.

In those days, there were very few grocery stores. General stores were usually the first retail establishments in the area with only a small selection of items. Most people raised their own livestock for meat, grew their own vegetables or bartered with their neighbors for whatever was needed. Catching fish was a nice way to add to a person's diet and a safe way for the children to help their families. Besides, fishing seemed more like fun than real work.

In the spring when the creeks were at their highest levels from the winter snow run off, children would secretly build a raft and see how far they could float down stream. There is just something attractive and fun about the water, whether you fish, raft, swim, or just sit on the bank day-dreaming as the water lazily floats by.

One Saturday afternoon three young boys secretly took a raft down to the creek that they'd built from the scrap lumber and logs they found on the floor of the nearby woods. The area had received several inches of rain recently and the creek was up almost to the top of the banks and flowing rapidly. The boys all knew how to swim, confident that if the raft tipped over they could easily swim to shore.

They didn't think about the speed of the current, any undercurrent, or that there were larger boulders in various parts of the stream just under the water level. All they thought about was having fun on the raft that they'd made all by themselves. Adventure was calling.

The raft was small; measuring only about four feet wide and five feet long. One boy sat cross-legged in the rear and used his paddle as a rudder to guide the craft. The other two boys sat on different sides to paddle when needed but usually the raft flowed just fine on its own. The current was strong enough to move the raft at a fast speed. The boys thought this was wonderful. They felt as if they could sail on to the ocean!

Everything went well for a time as the boys floated at a fairly gentle speed. Without realizing what was happening, the raft started to gather speed. Soon, it was going faster and faster. The boys grew nervous as the raft was floating rapidly out of control, though none of the boys would admit to being scared. They had no way to slow it down and were not able to steer the raft over to the bank.

The small "boat" continued to gather speed as the boys covered their mounting tension with talk and laughter, not paying attention to the current or the creek bed. Soon the creek took a sharp turn and at the same time the raft made contact with a large boulder that was just barely sticking out of the water.

When they collided with the boulder all three boys were thrown into the creek from the small unstable raft. Two of the boys were able to swim to the creek bed. But the third boy was thrown overboard, hit his head on the boulder, broke his neck and died instantly.

The two surviving boys were able to jump back into the water and pull their friend to shore. One of the boys ran for help while the other boy, crying uncontrollably, stayed by the creek with his dead friend cradled in his lap.

Neighbors rushed to the creek but nothing could be done to save the young boy. The other two boys soon became very quiet and, with their heads hanging low, slowly walked back to their homes, neither boy able to speak.

Most of the town turned out for the child's funeral. Every citizen wanted to do something to help the suffering family but no one was sure just what to do. How do you console a family who looses a son?

For days the two surviving boys stayed in seclusion not wanting to socialize with anyone. After a few months the boys each moved away from the area to live with relatives.

The parents of the deceased boy were so distraught that they decided to return to their relatives in Pennsylvania. Back then, it was impossible to transport a body any great distance; so the boy was buried in Ohio. In a small county cemetery, there is an unmarked grave for a young boy who died on a sunny Saturday afternoon while rafting with his friends. Few people know about it and many just hurry on by.

Young boys still raft down this creek. On sunny Saturday afternoons, a young boy is sometimes seen waving his arms and shouting, "Stop...stop...stop...stop! There's trouble ahead.... Stop....Stop!" Eerily, the boy is standing in the middle of the creek on top of the water! He continues to wave his arms until the new raft is steered over to the bank. Some have reported their raft moving towards the bank without being guided by the occupants – or was it? As soon as the raft aims toward the bank, the boy in the water fades away. After hearing about the tragedy involving the young boys, the occupants of the re-routed crafts often return to the creek to say a silent thank you to the boy who saved them.

Others tell of approaching the creek near the drowning location and seeing a young boy, waving his arms shouting, "Stop...stop...stop...stop! There's trouble ahead! Stop....stop!" This time the boy is standing on the bank. He continues to wave his arms until people leave the area or at least change their mind and decide not to swim.

No one ever swims in this section of the creek. Many people complain that when they are on the bank they feel too sad to swim or opt to just sit and stare at the creek in silence.

Can something good be the result of a child's death? You be the judge.

12. The High School

In rural Miami County were several three story brick school houses that were built in the very early 1900's. The building in this story was abandoned. In the 1950's, the baby boomers came into the population of Miami County and large school buildings were needed. Old buildings were often destroyed for a more modern, "better" facilities.

Like many such schools, this was a basic square shaped building with large windows on all four sides. Wooden double doors greeted visitors after they climbed several cement steps at the front entrance. Large, fierce looking gargoyles placed high on each corner of the structure glared down on the students as they arrived.

Creaky wooden floors were throughout the building. The hallways were lined with narrow metal lockers for the students, and each classroom had a wooden door with the top half containing a frosted piece of glass.

The basement had a storage area and the janitor's work room. Fred kept all his tools here and any item that was in need of repair. Fred had been the janitor for years. He was always the first person to arrive every morning and the last one to leave the building every evening. He attended all the school's sporting events, the plays, and the graduation ceremonies.

He liked to think that he had a part in the education of the kids and, in a way, he did. Fred always displayed an excellent work ethic for the students to follow and the example of a person taking pride in his work, no matter what the job. He believed that every job was important.

Occasionally Fred would help the boys with some project or give them advice on how to fix a car or a tractor. He was polite to the students and made sure that boys opened the doors for girls. He taught that good manners were also important.

Early one morning, Miss Meyer, the school principal, was walking down the hallway towards her office when she found Fred lying on the hallway floor. She ran quickly towards him but instantly knew that he was dead. Still, she checked for a pulse and found none. She removed her suit jacket and gently covered his face. The police, who were summoned while the students were kept out of the hallway, determined that Fred had died from a sudden heart attack.

The school was closed for a few days for the students to attend the funeral and try to absorb what had happened to Fred. A great sadness fell over the school. The rest of the year was covered by a blanket of grief. Fred had been like and respected and was missed by everyone.

Over the years students and teachers began to notice certain unexplained events were happening. If the door to a classroom was left opened, it wasn't long before unseen hands quietly closed it. If a teacher was ready to leave her classroom at the end of the day she might find her room door stuck tightly, and she was unable to leave. While thus delayed, she might notice that she'd forgotten to close one of the classroom windows. After the window was shut, she was able to exit the room without any problems at the door. On the way out, many would mumble, "Thank you, Fred."

Stubborn Spirits

The basement door was now always to be kept closed. The new janitor, James, found the door standing open one morning. He headed to the basement thinking that some students were up to mischief. Instead, James discovered that the furnace needed some attention in order to function properly. Fred was still taking care of his school.

As in most schools, the students were not allowed to run in the hallways. If the younger students galloped down the hall thinking that no one was watching, they soon saw an older man in overalls with his arms folded across his chest staring at the kids and mouthing the word "no running." Immediately the kids would stop running and the man would vanish. When the story was told, people all agreed that it was Fred keeping a watchful eye on the students.

The student population grew over the years and a new and larger school was soon needed. For several years this old building stood abandoned and neglected. Some people reported that when they walked past the old school at dusk they saw Fred standing at one of the windows looking out over the fields. If they came close to the building, they described the expression on Fred's face as one of sadness, as if he was looking for the kids.

When the decision was made to demolish the old school, the school board asked the current janitor to walk through the old building to make sure everything was removed that was worth saving. James started on the top floor, walking every hallway and checking in every room. At times he felt as if someone was watching him but he knew no one else was in the building.

By the time he was half-way through the top floor James thought he saw a man at the end of the hall dressed in coveralls and leaning against the wall. When James looked a second time the man was gone so James continued on with his job. After a while, James said softly "Why don't you walk with me Fred? This is more your school then it is mine."

For the rest of the inspection James felt as if he was working with someone.

James never explained why he would not allow anyone to walk through the building with him. When asked if he wanted help, James always answered, "We can do this." He never explained what he meant by "we."

Soon he was ready to go into the basement and check for any tools or equipment that needed to be removed. When James finished in the basement and headed for the stairs, he thought he heard someone softly crying, and then he saw a man sitting on the lower step dressed in coveralls, his elbows on his knees, and his head in his hands. James stopped in his tracks, not afraid, and said, "I'm so sorry Fred, I'm so sorry."

A couple of weeks later James was standing near the school watching the large equipment knock down the walls and haul the debris away to the local dump. He stood off to the side, avoiding the company of anyone else. If approached, James would softly smile and just move away.

James felt a sorrow come over him. He had attended school in this building and remembered Fred and how valuable and kind he was. Suddenly James felt a hand on his right shoulder, but when he turned his head, no one was visible. But James knew he was not alone – he knew that Fred was standing there beside him.

13. The Ghost Horse

During the early 1800's the Miami and Erie Canal was constructed beginning near Toledo and ending in Cincinnati at the Ohio River. Totaling around 250 miles of waterway, the canal was successful during that era in assisting with the transportation of goods and people throughout the state.

Many towns and businesses soon were established along the route providing food and lodging for the canal builders and later the travelers. The boatmen and the horses or mules that pulled the boats needed occasional protection from inclement weather. Soon docks and warehouses were constructed for the items being shipped. Think of this as the same development that now occurs along the current interstate highways and how almost every ramp has a gas station and a fast food restaurant.

As with any mode of transportation, tragedies sometimes occur. The canal boats were moved using horses or mules walking along on the canal bank harnessed to the boats with long ropes. Someone would be positioned on the rear of the boat to steer the vessel, a couple of people would be on each boat side using poles to help prevent the boat from bumping another boat and to help 'pole the boat' or push it along. A final person would walk along behind the animal, holding the lines and encouraging the animal on.

In the first half of the 1800's, the canal was an excellent way to transport goods and provide a means of travel. It also created serious temptation for certain people to take advantage of others.

Animals were the most important part of this travel. Every few miles the boats needed to stop so that the crewmen could rest the horses. If there was a station near the canal, the driver could change his horse for a rested one and continue on his way. Without a strong healthy animal, the canal boats could not cover much distance.

People working or traveling on the boats also needed to stop occasionally to rest and to eat a meal. If a person was lucky there would be a station where they could sleep in a bed for the night.

One evening in 1827, a canal boat was making its way toward Cincinnati loaded with furs from Canada. Somehow a rumor spread that under the furs was a large shipment of gold and silver headed for a bank in Cincinnati.

Some would rather steal than actually work. A plot was soon developed by three men of dubious character, to rob the canal boat of all its goods. The thieves were sure that they would become instantly rich and famous and live the rest of their lives in the luxury they felt they deserved.

The robbers waited all day in the hot sun and finally, just after dusk as a cloudy night developed, the boat came slowly into view. It seemed to be the perfect time and location for them to attack the boat. The boat came into sight unaware of what fate awaited the crew and passengers. Two robbers were stationed on the east bank, hiding in thick woods with the third on the west bank behind some shrubs.

Unknown to the two robbers on the east bank, the third partner, who was alone, fell asleep behind the shrub and did not see the boat approaching. Suddenly, loud gun fire erupted, piercing the air, and screaming from the crew broke the silence of the evening. Hiding on the boat under the huge pile of furs were four sharpshooters hired to protect the shipment.

The two thieves on the east bank were not good shots and soon the boat was full of holes and the lines to the horse were cut by stray bullets. The horse ran wildly from the scene and trampled the robber on the west bank to death while he fumbled for his rifle. The boat soon took on water and sank to the bottom of the canal.

The east bank thieves were shot to death in the hail of gunfire. The four hired gunman reached the bank in safety with no passenger casualties on the boat. Eventually the furs and gold were salvaged from the water.

The local authorities were summoned and soon the evening's events were sorted out and three dead bodies were taken away by the sheriff.

The robbers were buried by the sheriff's department and were soon forgotten. They had no identification and the local residents cared little about identifying the men that had caused so much damage. Conversely, the four guards were considered heroes for protecting the money and saving the crew.

By the mid 1850's train companies started laying tracks in the area and soon the Miami Erie Canal was no longer used for transportation. Parts of the canal were filled in and buildings were constructed. Some towns along the canal continued to thrive and grow while others slowly became ghost towns.

There is a location in Warren County, near where the canal used to flow, that on a quiet night shortly after dusk you can hear the sound of a horse stomping and running in terror with the reins jingling wildly. Some people claimed to have heard the screams of a horrified man as if he were being beaten or stomped to death. Others have reported the smell of gunpowder though no one fired a weapon.

The site on which an old school building was built (now demolished for a new structure) had a history of strange events. This building stood on the spot where the attempted canal boat robbery occurred years ago.

Stubborn Spirits

A spot on the ground surrounding the building was never able to grow anything. It was the exact location where the robber had been trampled to death. Students planted trees and shrubs in this area, but they all quickly died.

Young children who attended the school did not like to be on the playground at dusk because they felt as if someone was watching them. Some children complained of hearing a loud bang, like a gun shot, but the source of the noise was never found. The adults patrolled the area around the building but found nothing.

After the school was torn down, construction workers often complained that someone was moving their hand tools around at night. This only happened in one location of the building site so the workers just avoided this area and nothing else was moved. When the workers were required to work late they stayed away from this spot because sometimes they could detect the faint smell of gunpowder in the air.

A couple of times the workers heard a faint scream for help in this area but could find no one. On a few mornings they noticed hoof prints in the dirt though it would have been impossible for anyone to have ridden through the securely locked, fenced-in area. As dusk approached, the men would hear the sounds of a horse walking past and the slap of the reins as if a horse was being driven.

The location of the old school is now a parking lot with nothing reported in recent years. How sad.

Stubborn Spirits

14. The Need for Speed

There are stretches of narrow country roads where very few semi trucks and only a scattering of cars travel. These roadways connect two small rural towns and except for residents, there is no reason to use such an out-of-the-way route. The roadways are lined with farmhouses, pastures with livestock, and, of course, crops. These county roads dip and rise like ribbon candy. Driving down the winding old roads can be relaxing for the soul, but you can't look at the scenery for too long because these county lanes have plenty of sharp, dangerous curves.

Preble County is home to the perfect county road. The farms are beautiful and well kept with skillfully tended fields showing few weeds to interfere with the crops. On one side of the road a large stream flows for a few miles with clear, clean water just waiting for someone with a fishing pole.

This road was used for years with very few accidents. Most travelers were farmers going into town or moving their equipment from field to field. It was not unusual to see a 4-H member riding his horse along the side of the road, enjoying the day.

Very few highway signs were posted to warn motorists about the sharp curves or when to slow down, but local residents were aware of the dangers. In the era before seat belts and air bags, speed was not always important to people, but safety was.

In the 1950's the desire for speed and muscle cars seemed to skyrocket. It was the post World War II era and people were living life to the fullest, working at good jobs and wanting to enjoy their income. Lonely back country roads offered a way to test driving skills and to see just how fast those muscle cars could move. At least that was the thinking of teenagers in the 50's, many of whom worked after school and at summer jobs in order to purchase their first jalopy.

On a sunny fall Saturday afternoon, two good friends were out driving in Jim's new Chevy. Jim had picked up his new used car at the dealership that morning. When not in school or working, teen-aged boys worked on their cars to soup up the engine or just to fancy up the car to impress the other kids.

Jim was cruising along the road with the top down, enjoying the sunny afternoon. The car radio was turned to the local rock-n-roll station, not blaring but at a level that allowed talking between the two close friends. The boys were discussing their double dates that evening and where they would go for pizza after the evening movie. They were also eager for the fall harvest to begin so they could earn some money for college by working for Jim's grandfather who owned a large nearby farm.

Jim was talking and listening to the beat of the music before he realized that he was approaching the upcoming curve too fast. He suddenly hit the brakes hard causing the car to spin wildly out of control. The tires squealed, leaving long black skid marks on the blacktop, and causing smoke to rise from the tires. Skidding sideways, Jim's new car rolled several times down the embankment into the river, landing on its top just in the edge of the water. The radio continued to play popular music loudly while the tires, sticking straight up in the air, continued to spin around and around.

Both boys had been ejected from the car and suffered horrible injuries. They lay on the ground as the radio continued to play. The car was now a mangled mess of steel with parts strewn everywhere.

A farmer mowing in a near-by field rushed to the scene to see if he could help the occupants. Before getting close to the car, he feared the boys had broken their necks. The horrible injuries to their faces made them unrecognizable. The closer he got, there was no doubt that they were dead.

The farmer quickly jumped on his tractor and droved back to his house to summon the county sheriff. He had a strange, heartrending feeling on the drive home as he thought about the suffering to be endured by the families of the dead victims. Though their injuries were so bad that he had not recognized them, the strange, disturbing feeling persisted. Why was this crash scene affecting him so much?

Later that day, the farmer learned that the boy driving the red Chevy convertible was his grandson, his only grandson. The old man was devastated. He loved that boy.

He had hoped the grandson would someday take over the farming operation.

For years the farmer would drive out of his way to avoid that curve in the road. He never fished in that river again and, in fact, he did his best to avoid even looking at the river. He never mowed that field again. The vision of the mangled bodies stayed with the farmer for the rest of his life, as did the imagined sounds of a horrible crash.

People walking on that stretch of road still hear the sounds of tires squealing, 50's rock-n-roll and metal being torn apart in a crash. And if they remain standing still after they hear the sound of the crash, they hear soft weeping; the cry of a broken heart. The sound comes from the near-by field that has not been mowed in years. No one is ever seen in that field but there is no denying the sound of crying.

Now there are highway reflector signs on both sides of the roadway warning about the upcoming curve. Fortunately there has not been a wreck at this location for years, because of the signs and the knowledge of the road's tragic history.

If your car is speeding down this road on a sunny fall afternoon, you just might see the faint vision of a teenager on the side of the road waving both arms high over his head as if to warn people to stop or at least slow down. His hair is styled in a 50's ducktail, his blue jeans' cuffs turned up, and his loafers have pennies in the top. If you look at his face you will see sadness in his eyes.

Stop the car and the vision will fade away right before your eyes. Turn off the engine and listen. From the unattended field behind you will be the sound of heart wrenching crying, the saddest crying you will ever hear. Look carefully, because no one is in that field!

People who see the boy beside the road slow down and say "Thanks Jim."

15. The Broken Heart

In the early 1800's, transportation was a major problem for the Ohio area settlers. The roadways were only dirt paths except for the few heavily traveled ones where the earth was packed hard as cement. The most frequently used streets had deep ruts created by the wagon wheels that made travel slow and bumpy and caused damage to the goods being transported.

Movement of supplies was time consuming and dangerous and travel for a person was nearly impossible. Travelers had to contend with the weather, the fact that there were few shelters for an over night stay, and the danger of bandits who were eager to steal the goods to resell or to rob the travelers of any valuable personal items.

Between 1825 and 1845 the Miami and Erie Canal were constructed extending from Toledo to Cincinnati, Ohio. This was a huge accomplishment with no heavy earth moving equipment. All the work was done by hand with shovels, picks, and only wheelbarrows to remove the dirt and hard-

115

packed clay. The hot humid summer weather followed by harsh cold winters made the work demanding.

The canal was four feet deep and approximately forty feet wide with a ten foot wide tow path on each side for horses or mules to assist with the movement of the boats.

When the canal was completed in the 1840's, the railroad was just beginning to expand into Ohio and competition for passengers and supplies was fierce. The trains proved to be faster, safer, and carried people to more parts of the state than the canal, which ran around 250 miles in length. The railroads already had approximately 3,000 miles of tracks in Ohio by the 1860's.

Various feeder lakes adjacent to the canal supplied it with a constant flow of water. The early 1800's was a very different time period than today. With a large number of men constantly working together, near and/or immersed in filthy water, disease became common and widespread. Healthcare for people was limited to whatever the workers could do for themselves. Hygiene was almost non-existent due to a lack of facilities for individual needs, and people had little knowledge concerning personal care.

The workers' diet came both from whatever food the company was able to barter for with the local farmers and from any game hunted by hired company scouts. Sometimes the men had meat to eat, but usually it was just watery soup from various plants that grew wild in the area. They worked long hard hours, usually from dawn to dusk six days a week and they slept on the ground at night using whatever makeshift shelter they could find. The conditions were difficult, but the men were just glad to have a job.

Violence was a common problem. In those days, people would just ask the boss for a job and it was either a yes or no. There were no applications or background checks performed. Therefore, a convict could be working beside a minister who was trying to supplement his small income from his church.

Many of the men visited the nearest town on their one day off looking for fun, women, and drink. Some of the men brought back alcohol and a deck of cards, both of which were forbidden in the work camp. Drunken fights would occasionally break out among the men and fatal shootings were the usual way to settle the dispute.

If a man died from violence, disease, or a work related accident he was usually buried somewhere nearby, but not always in a cemetery. If the authorities could locate the next of kin, the family would determine where the deceased was to be buried. Many shallow graves line various areas along the canal route due to the fact that most families had little money and could not afford to have the body transported back home.

As the canal faded from use, sections of the waterway were filled with dirt and debris. Soon people and towns bought parts of the canal, filled them in, and erected a building or converted the land to farming.

In recent years many sections of the canal have been reconstructed and become tourist attractions with actual canal boats or nice areas for hiking. In Miami County there are beautiful areas where people can walk along the exact location of the old canal that used to provide the only transportation to the area.

On a quiet day as you walk along the old tow path you may hear the sound of shovels clanking against rocks and the swish of dirt being thrown into a wheelbarrow. When you look around you will discover that no one else is there. You take a few more steps and again you hear the sound of shovels digging and throwing dirt. Once again, no one else is around. There is no need to run away because these are the sounds of the canal being constructed.

If you get up the nerve to tell your friends about the sounds you heard, they will tell you that you have heard the workers continuing to build the canal since they have heard the same sounds many times. They sit on the canal banks, close their eyes and imagine a bye-gone era.

Some people have spent time sitting on the dried out bank of the old empty canal in an isolated area. They swear that they can smell the water and hear it lapping against the shore. Needless to say, some people quickly leave the area and hurry back to their cars, but then, they realize that there is nothing to fear, and return to the bank hoping to hear the sounds again.

There is one area, in southern Miami County that on a quiet, still day you may hear the horrifying screams of several men and then, suddenly silence. This is the location where four men died due to a sudden cave in. These unfortunate men were digging the base of the canal with shovels. Sadly, they were not careful where they tossed the removed dirt and soon a huge mound had formed near the edge of the canal. The ground became unstable and the men were quickly buried under several feet of dirt with no chance of survival.

In another area of the county, several people have reported seeing a man dressed in old time work clothes, running along the towpath beside the canal but they do not hear his footsteps. It's impossible to tell if he's running from or to something. Several people have reported seeing him and they all felt the slight breeze as he ran past them but no one heard his footsteps. Perhaps he was running to help the men in the collapsed ditch.

In a rural area of Miami County, an alleged haunting that has been reported since the mid nineteenth century is a good tale. Sara was to be married on her family's farm in the 1840's to a canal boat pilot. She met the captain on a hot, humid summer day when he stopped the boat to rest the horses. From that day forward, she watched for the boat and waved at the captain. Soon he would stop the boat at least weekly to spend time with Sara. A romance quickly developed between the pair and the happy couple became engaged.

The wedding was to be held near the canal. She told her friends, "It will be perfect. We'll be married on the farm where I grew up and near the canal where my future husband earns his living!"

The happy day arrived bright and sunny. Sara dressed in her white wedding dress and wore the hand made veil that her deceased mother had worn many years earlier. The guests had arrived and everyone was on the lawn waiting for the ceremony to begin. Sara's minister, a long time family friend, was there to marry the couple.

They waited and waited. Soon everyone started talking in a whisper not sure what to do. How long should they wait? Should they quietly go home? What do you say to the bride?

Sadly the groom did not show up. Quietly her family and friends left for their homes leaving Sara and her father alone. Sara soon retreated upstairs to her bedroom inconsolable. She silently sat in the rocking chair looking out the window towards the canal. She never shed a tear, just sat gazing at the canal.

Stubborn Spirits

Three months later Sara was found dead in her father's home, dressed in her white dress and wearing the hand made veil. The doctor determined that she died of natural causes. Her family always believed that she died of a broken heart.

Over the years there have been several sightings of a lady dressed in white wearing a beautiful veil walking along the canal path. Her hands are shading her eyes from the bright sunshine and she is watching the water as she looks around the people. People who have seen her say that she appears to be looking for someone because she walks past them without a glance.

When people look at her face, they see extreme sadness but no tears. People report their feelings of wanting to comfort or help the lady in white but when they approach her she quietly disappears!

Over the years the house has had dozens of owners. Many people have reported strange feelings if they stay in the upstairs bedroom where Sara died. The most recent family to own this house has used Sara's bedroom for storage because no one will occupy that particular room. People say that they feel as if the room is already occupied and its inhabitant does not want to be disturbed.

The canal boat captain was never seen or heard from again.

Stubborn Spirits

16. The Misunderstanding

On a beautiful spring day, sixteen year old Marybeth and her Dad were out walking on their family farm. Eventually they made their way down to the creek where they often shared many afternoons fishing. Marybeth looked over at a large boulder that sat under a large shade tree and she instantly stopped walking. She grabbed her father's arm and whispered, "Who is that girl sitting on the rock?"

"That's just Catherine Miller," he replied. Marybeth turned to her father with a quizzical expression. "I guess it's time for you to learn the story about Catherine and the history of our farm," he said. They walked a short distance away from the rock and sat down on the bank by the creek. During the telling, Marybeth cast several glances back to the boulder, looking for the elusive Catherine.

For years, Warren County was mainly an agricultural area. Then in the 1950's and 1960's the neighboring population in Montgomery County experienced a huge population growth and the need for more housing quickly became apparent. Soon the citizens of Warren County began to build houses in their undeveloped beautiful county, but our story takes place years before this suburban sprawl.

Like many counties in this part of Ohio, Warren County is blessed with rolling terrain and creeks of clear flowing water which, in the 1800's, provided water for the livestock and the settlers. And now the creeks are the sources of eerie stories great for the telling.

In the 1840's several farms were well established along the Todd Fork Creek. The Millers had lived in this location for several years and were known for raising healthy livestock and harvesting a good grain crop. Ten children were born to the Millers and all were fortunate to live past infancy, which was most unusual in the 1840's.

As the family grew, the size of the farm also grew. The Millers cut down all the trees needed for the buildings and had the local mill saw the logs into usable lumber for the construction needs. Soon there were several barns and corrals constructed for the livestock.

Mr. Miller provided for his family by adding on to the log cabin as the need developed. The entire family helped with the building of the cabin additions and everyone enjoyed having a part in the construction.

For cooking, the family used a heavy black iron stove which was heated by burning small pieces of chopped wood. The younger children were always taught to stay away from the stove as the entire fixture would be very hot when in use. There was the constant danger of hands being burned or maybe clothing catching on fire.

A large stone fireplace made with smooth stones from the nearby creek was located in the main room and heated the entire cabin during the winter. Danger from a fireplace was always a concern as sparks from the burning wood could jump out onto the wood cabin floor or onto a woman's long dress if she walked too close to the fire. In those days, ladies' long full dresses often ignited, sometimes with fatal results.

The younger Miller children spent many happy hours playing on the homestead as they grew up. Until the children were old enough to handle the small chores, they were allowed plenty of play time. One of their favorite spots was down by the nearby creek, but always under the supervision of an older child or adult.

The youngest daughter had a favorite rock where she loved to sit with her feet dangling in the water. A large spreading maple tree stood nearby providing cool shade on the humid summer days. She considered this her special rock and did not want anyone else to sit there.

One weekend, young Catherine was allowed to spend a Saturday with her best friend who lived on a neighboring farm. She was to come home after church on Sunday. These neighbors had been personal friends of the Millers for years. Both families helped each other throughout the decades with farm chores or the yearly butchering and any other jobs that required assistance. Sadly, that Saturday night the neighbor's cabin burned to the ground with no survivors! The young Miller girl died with her best friend.

The Millers suffered through tremendous grief at the lost of their daughter and that of their neighbors. They mourned at the church cemetery with the rest of the town's citizens as all of the victims were buried a couple of days later.

The farm remained in the Miller family well into the twentieth century. The cabin was eventually replaced with a sturdy white frame two story house. During World War II, Betty, a female descendent of the Millers, lived alone in the old family homestead and maintained the farm herself.

Betty had dated a young man, Josiah, from her church for several years before he went off to war. They became very fond of each other and spent many Sunday afternoons on picnics and visiting with friends. The courtship was very proper; church functions or walking about the town were the main activities for dating. Betty was a little shy and rarely talked about herself or her family but she always enjoyed Josiah's companionship. Betty and Josiah spent hours talking and planning their future together on the farm.

When the time arrived for Josiah to leave, she promised that she would wait for him and that she would write weekly. As they tearfully hugged and gently shared their first kiss good-bye at the train station, the promises were repeated and repeated. Tears were shed by both as they waved good-bye.

The train slowly pulled out of the station with Josiah hanging out the window waving good bye and shouting, "I love you!" Betty blew kisses to Josiah and stood staring on the platform long after the train faded into the distance.

Two years and many letters later, luckily for the young soldier, he survived the war without any injuries. After being discharged from the Army, Josiah quickly returned home on his newly purchased surplus Army motorcycle to join his waiting girlfriend. His one true love! His only love! Soon he would see his love and they would never, never be separated again.

He just knew from her letters that she had been faithful and decided to surprise her. Not telling her the exact date that he would return, he happily headed home with love and marriage on his mind. As he came closer to the farm he waved in greeting at the neighbors that he knew and shouted that he was going to surprise Betty.

On a balmy, sunny afternoon, with her surprise engagement ring safely in his pants pocket, he joyfully rode up the dirt driveway to the house and his special love. The motorcycle screeched to a stop and he quickly turned off the engine.

He raced up the front porch steps and in his excitement opened the screen door without knocking. Josiah took a step into the house, shouted her name, "Betty, Betty" only to find her clutched in the arms of another man! The shock on his face rendered him speechless. He clumsily stumbled backward out the front door, fell down the porch steps, staggered and ran all at the same time to his bike.

Jumping on the motorcycle he revved the engine several times and fiercely stared for just a second at Betty who had run out onto the porch calling out Josiah's name. Betty did not realize that the man who held her in a hug seconds before was now standing behind her. Josiah took off roaring down the driveway at top speed while she was yelling for him to stop. Josiah never looked back!

Betty was never given the opportunity to explain that this was her cousin who, with his wife and children, had just arrived for a weekend visit!

Not paying attention to where he was driving, Josiah sped down the road and started across the nearby bridge. In his blind anger the young soldier was not really looking at the roadway or the bridge and sadly drove over the side of the bridge flying into the creek to his instant death.

Did he loose control of the bike or did he drive off the bridge on purpose is a question that never has been answered. This question does not need an answer. The very sad result is that this soldier had survived a war to die once reaching his home.

No one knows exactly what happened or why but the motorbike broke into several pieces on impact with the headlight flying off to rest by itself in the water. Josiah's head was severed from his body. Neither the light, nor poor Josiah's head was ever found.

Over the years if a person approached the bridge from the old Miller homestead they just may have seen the wandering vision of a jilted lover standing near the creek looking sadly at the house.

Some people reported hearing the sound of crying coming from the creek, but the source was never found. A few individuals saw a man walking along the creek away from the house carrying a head under his arm.

People strolling along the creek have heard the sound of a motorcycle crossing the bridge. As the sound of the engine grows louder and louder, folks quickly walk away from the bridge and then suddenly, hear the noise of something splashing into the water. No vehicle is ever seen!

At night when someone is walking across the old bridge, they have reported sightings of a bright light as if it were coming from the creek like a beam of a spotlight shining up into the air! When people search the creek the next day they can never find the light source.

Betty soon moved from the area out to Montana to live with some relatives. She was never heard from again.

~

As for Catherine Miller, who died in the neighboring fire, most believe she is still on the old farm. She has been sighted several times by the creek sitting on the shady boulder that was her favorite spot. As you approach her, you may hear her soft mournful crying and then she'll slowly turn her head, look at you and softly whisper just one word: "Why?"

17.   The Buffalo Skull and Betrayal

Driving down one of the many country roads in Preble County during a moonlit night you just may see the strangest sight that you have ever seen. Standing on the edge of the creek is a beautiful stately buffalo taking a long slow drink of water!

Areas of this county, throughout history, were battlegrounds over the land. Fights between the soldiers and Native Americans and even the native wildlife were common in the 1700's. None of the battles are featured in text books or in the movies, but they were important to the settlement of the area.

As new Americans were encouraged to move west during the development of the country, the lure of cheap land and the thrill of adventure drove many people in that direction. Very little thought was given to the original settlers – The Native Americans. Some of the newcomers decided that they could just move in and take over. The Indians were swiftly forced to move on west, and the wildlife that had roamed the territory for generations was killed in large numbers.

People finally decided that the area was being over-hunted when there was only one buffalo left in the county. The settlers named him Creek because he was usually seen down at the creek in the evening getting a long drink of water. The locals all agreed to never kill him and let him live out his days.

In the very early 1800's some French soldiers were passing through the area on their way to what is now Canada. One of the Frenchmen spotted the buffalo at the creek and shot him dead.

The angered settlers soon attacked the French soldiers, who were eating buffalo meat in their camp. Every French soldier was killed. While one of the attackers took all of the valuables from the dead, another man found the buffalo skull, cleaned it carefully, and then placed all the French soldiers' valuables in the skull. This was then buried nearby. Over the years many stories have evolved about buried treasure but this stash of valuables has never been found!

~

Along this same creek around dusk you can hear the sound of a person or persons jumping into the creek. But when you look for the source of the sound no one is there.

Shortly before the beginning of the Civil War a family moved into the area in the hopes of establishing a church. The man had been a pastor back east and was excited about bringing the Word to the new territory. .

Soon the couple and their three children began farming to provide a steady income for the family. The pastor traveled around the area encouraging people to attend prayer services in their one room cabin. He was well received and soon the small congregation grew to a size requiring that the services be held in a local barn until a new structure could be built.

That building was used as a schoolhouse during the week and a church on Sundays. The minister was proud of the growth of his church family and continued to drive his buggy around the area, visiting any new arrivals and spreading the Word.

During one of his trips around the territory, he met a beautiful young widow. Soon a friendship developed and, before long, an intimacy grew between the couple. After the first indiscretion, the pastor stopped on his way home and prayed for forgiveness. He promised himself that he would never stray again.

He vowed not to visit the widow unless he had another member of the church with him. This private rule of his lasted for only a few weeks. Then on a hot humid afternoon, while out slowly driving his buggy, he came across the young widow walking home from town. Being a kind person, he offered her a ride, secretly telling himself to be careful.

He drove her back to her house and was invited in for cold drink of water. After a short hesitation, he agreed to rest his tired horse and to sit on the shady porch. The couple visited for awhile, enjoying the cold refreshing water.

When the minister stood up to leave, the widow gave him an inviting, sensual hug and shortly he found himself kissing her. Soon the kiss deepened and she responded to his touch. The couple quickly moved inside the small house and quickly to the widow's bed, eagerly making tender love to each other.

Overcome with guilt, the minister quickly dressed without speaking to the widow. He hitched his horse to the buggy and left at a fast trot for somewhere, anywhere far away from the scene of his betrayal. He had some thinking and praying to do. Yet, he found that he was not angry with her – in fact, he wanted to return to her arms. He asked himself, "Why was he thinking about the widow and not his family?"

Again the minister prayed for forgiveness on his way home but he knew that he had fallen for the widow and wanted to spend more and more time with her. Though his sin was a burden, he felt powerless to stop seeing his young lover. Hoping that no one would ever discover the truth about these pastoral visits, he continued the regular afternoon trysts.

After a few months, the pastor's wife began to notice a change in her husband's attitude towards her and the children. He seemed distant from her and rarely returned her affection. Even when he did, his wife could tell that his mind was elsewhere. He often came home more relaxed than expected after visiting his congregation. He had always been excited about meeting new people and possible new members for the church and seemed happy to see the children. He remained polite to his family, maybe too polite.

Her suspicions got the best of her one day, so the pastor's wife saddled a horse to follow her husband's buggy at a safe distance. She watched him enter the widow's cabin rather than sit on the porch and enjoy the cool breeze.

Dismounting from her horse she sat on the ground in the nearby woods, resting her head on her drawn up knees. The moments stretched into minutes and then to hours as she pondered what to do. She never thought anything like this would happen to her. She was stunned; vacillating between total shock and fury beyond control and then, back to shock.

As the afternoon stretched on, she thought about the children and all the years together with her husband. They had worked so hard to live on a minister's salary. She had raised their children and worked even harder to earn extra money by selling eggs from their few chickens so that he could continue to make his "church visits." There was no stopping the bitter tears that ran down her face as she sat huddled in the woods.

From her hiding place, she saw the cabin door open and the couple emerge from inside. She watched them embrace on the porch, then meet in a warm, lingering kiss and then another before finally pulling reluctantly apart.

The poor woman snapped. She quickly jumped up on her horse and raced toward the couple, screaming in her anguish and chasing them towards the creek. Her husband and his lover fled before her, holding hands as they ran, crying and begging her for mercy. When they reached the creek, they stumbled into the water, both of them hitting their heads on the submerged rocks, and drowned.

The jilted wife slowed her horse to a walk and looked down at the couple. The tears stopped as she stared at the her husband and his lover floating face down in the water.. She felt no sorrow for them or herself; in fact, she was not sure if she felt any emotion at all. Her only thought concerned how to explain to the children what had happened and why.

Church members believed that she was justified in her anger and no one wanted any charges filed against the minister's wife. The congregation unanimously agreed to refuse the minister and his lover a Christian burial. Their bodies were removed from the creek and buried in shallow graves in the woods. The deceased woman's cabin was sold and the money was given to the minister's new widow to help support her children.

Over the years, when people sat beside the creek on a sunny afternoon, they heard screaming followed by a splashing sound. They saw large ripples in the water as if someone had just jumped in, but no one was there. Others report hearing the sound of a horse racing at top speed toward the creek, with no animal in sight.

As dusk approaches, the image of a large buffalo appears beside the same creek with his head down taking a long drink of water. Slowly, the solitary beast vanishes into thin air.

Not far from the creek where two different tragedies occurred is an old forgotten cemetery. Currently it is surrounded by corn and soy bean fields and accessible only by driving down a narrow dirt lane. Very few people visit this cemetery and usually it is only those interested in history or genealogy research. There are only a few remaining tombstones most of which are faded from years of weather exposure.

One monument has no name or dates; just the image of a woman's face carved into the stone. Rumor has it that the family of the beautiful young widow secretly removed her body from its shallow grave in the woods one night and quietly buried her in this lonely cemetery. For many years, there was no tombstone as the family feared someone would steal or vandalize the marker. They knew that the church members blamed her for leading the minister into sin, but they could not live with the idea of her being abandoned in the woods.

Some report that they've walked past this grave and seen tears running down the stone face of the beautiful, lonely widow.

18.   Screams and Voices of the U.G.R.R.

Have you ever heard of a railroad with no tracks? In the 1800's Darke County had the U.G.R.R.-- The Underground Railroad. And you can still hear the screams and voices along the old route.

West of Greenville, Ohio, is a large area of farmland that played an important part in the Underground Railroad. During the late 1780's a settlement began here that would remain active for nearly one hundred years. This community was attractive to a wide variety of people which eventually included folks whose ancestry included Negro, European, and Native American descent.

When the Underground Railroad began to develop and grow, this community quickly became known as an important station on the railroad line. A nearby settlement of Quakers helped to support this town, where the escaped slaves could find shelter, food, and hopefully, safety before they continued on with their journey.

Throughout the 1800's as the number of slaves in the South grew, the number of fleeing slaves also grew. Many of them only stayed for a short time in Ohio because they feared for their lives. They quickly continued on in their flight toward Canada.

The slaves who traveled the railroad usually arrived during the night. They were escorted to shelter, given food and allowed to rest as long as needed. Then when the time was right, they were helped along further North toward their destination always under the cover of darkness.

Some of the escaped slaves decided to settle here, doing their best to blend in with the community and keep a low profile. Many became prominent citizens and gave their assistance to other slaves hoping for freedom.

Many slaves traveling the railroad were tired and weary and once they reached Ohio they gave up the fight to travel on and settled here. Others were not in good health and passed away while resting in this community.

Not everything was perfect in the settlement. Some of the Southern slave owners sent bounty hunters after their "property." There is at least one documented occasion where the hunters entered the settlement looking for run away slaves. They searched several cabins and barns looking for anyone with a bounty. You can imagine the horror and fear that went through the town! The screams pierced the quiet night air as each person did their best to fight off the bounty hunters.

The community became an active abolitionist stronghold and when people of color were allowed to become soldiers during the Civil War, some of the young men from this community joined the Massachusetts 54th, the first colored regiment. Some of these veterans returned to their adopted Darke County homes and are buried in the local cemeteries.

Over the years the buildings in the settlement either collapsed or people demolished them not realizing their importance to the history of this area and the country. Only a few of the original structures remain. Most reflect the typical style of the early 1800's: red brick squares, one or two stories high and one room log cabin homes. This mix of dwellings is typical of any community in development during that time.

At its peak this town reached a population of about five hundred people. Many of these families led normal lives, living on their farms and raising their children. A high mortality rate was also normal. Wives died during childbirth, children died from various untreatable diseases, and some just passed away from the harsh life.

Today's residents have reported visions of adults and children who are walking around the remaining buildings or looking out of the windows of the standing structures, watching for someone. Whenever the living approached them, they vanished into the air.

There are also reports of a soldier in a Union uniform marching back and forth as if guarding a building. No one is sure what he is protecting, but he remains on duty.

At other times, a soft crying can be heard. It is uncertain whether the tears are caused by sorrow or from joy at finally reaching the land of freedom. It is difficult to imagine the feeling the escaped slaves had when they reached the North and their dreams became reality.

A few people have heard fearful, terrifying screams during the night: the kind that causes a shiver to run down your spine and you hair to stand on end. This is soon followed by a loud wailing as if someone were being chased and was in imminent danger of being killed!

No structures have been added to this area for years. The last new building was abandoned years ago without explanation by the owner. Since that time a few visitors have walked around the building during the daytime and all had reported hearing soft voices, as if people are praying. The source of the voices is never found. Newspaper clippings from years ago report that citizens held prayer meetings in their houses during the afternoon. Could be the prayer meetings are still in session.

19. Death Returns Again

In a small Preble County town stands a red brick building that's two stories high with a large loading dock out back. The design was narrow and long, typical of businesses 100 years ago. There are creaky wooden steps leading to a basement lined with stone walls that rest upon a hard packed dirt floor. The business started in the late 1800's as a general store and served the community for several years.

This store had been the most popular place for residents to shop and the best place to learn what was happening around the community. Folks could shop for clothing, groceries and seed for the farm, or order parts for farm equipment or home furnishings. Most important, it was the local post office. General stores and churches were often good sources of information because if these cities had a newspaper it was probably only printed once a week.

Lucas, the store's owner, always contributed money to local school campaigns, church fund-raising events, and other worthwhile community causes. He did this because he loved his community and wanted to do whatever he could to help it develop. The local citizens loved to shop at his store, not only because it stocked a wide variety of goods but also because the store was a strong supporter of their town.

Lucas and his wife always worked together in the store. As their children grew up they worked with their parents, making this a true family business.

One day during the 1930's the owner's wife suddenly collapsed while working at the store. Immediately, Lucas sent someone for the doctor and waited on the floor beside his wife, holding her hand and pleading with her not to leave him. Over and over he said, "Don't go, don't go, don't go." She took her final breathe as Lucas sat helplessly by. The town doctor rushed to the store, but she had already passed on. He declared her death to be from unknown heart problems.

Working through his grief the owner sadly continued to operate the store, but Lucas never felt so lonely in all his life. He found some comfort in his family, his church, and his friends, but no one could ever replace his wife – his partner, his true soul mate.

His daughter and son began helping him fulltime with the business, all three trying to cope with the loss of a wife and mother. Soon the threesome developed a good working routine and life became more bearable for Lucas. Once again, Lucas was able to enjoy living.

A couple of years later the owner's only daughter, Isabel, was walking down the basement stairs, which she had done hundreds and hundreds of times over the years. She missed a step and tumbled to her death.

Again the owner suffered greatly and with the help of his son, their friends, and his church, Lucas was able to continue to manage the store. After several weeks Lucas slowly began to enjoy life again but always under a cloud of sadness. He wondered how much sadness a person must endure and why.

In the late 1930's the owner's son, Mark, was drafted into the Army. At that time the country was at peace and Lucas did not worry too much for his son's well being. He expected that the boy would be gone around three years and then return home and help run the store. Then, some day, his son would take over the store from his father much as Lucas had done with his father.

While Mark was in the Army, Lucas hired a couple of older men to help out with the store. Each man only wanted to work part time because they both had farms to operate, but they knew that this would provide some much needed extra money during the hard times of the Depression. Lucas did enjoy the companionship of men his own age, so it worked out well.

In 1941, Lucas received a letter from his son telling him that he was currently stationed in Hawaii at a base named Pearl Harbor. Lucas wrote back, telling Mark to enjoy the sunshine and warm weather because it was so different from Ohio's weather. Still, Lucas did not worry about him, thinking what a nice, pleasant, place Pearl Harbor must be.

The attack at Pearl Harbor on December, 1941, forced his son to serve longer than three years. Fortunately, the boy survived the long difficult war and returned home healthy and ready to work at the store he loved. The son looked a little older and was more serious about life but otherwise Lucas could not see anything different either mentally or physically about him.

After World War II, when shopping malls began to pop up and people started driving further distances for their supplies, business at the store began to decline. Sadly, the general store finally closed its doors due to a lack of business. Many citizens asked Lucas and Mark to stay open because the store had always been there; yet they continued to drive to the nearby mall. Father and son debated long and hard about what to do. They loved the store and the work involved but knew it could no longer provide a living for them.

After the store was closed for the final time, the son returned alone later that night. Mark walked into the backroom, threw a rope over the center rafter, carefully placed the noose around his neck and jumped off the high stack of feed sacks. He survived the war but could not survive the changing times of the country.

That was how Lucas found his son – swinging slowly back and forth, back and forth. The only sound to be heard was the creaking of the rope as his boy swung slowly back and forth. Neither birds singing in the distance, nor the brightly shining sun could reach Lucas over the sound of the swinging rope that held his son.

The next day Lucas returned to the store to retrieve some papers from the desk which sat in the corner of the backroom. There on the desk was a hand written note to Lucas from his son. It read "I just don't understand it. After fighting for my country, the local people decided to shop elsewhere. I only wanted to work here and keep the family tradition going. Why did the people leave us? Why? Why?"

Lucas cried and cried. He cried until he had no more tears though his chest continued to heave in dry sobs. He cried until he was physically sick; he was utterly alone. His entire family was now at the local cemetery – without him. The silence of the store was over whelming, so slowly, with a heavy step and his head down, Lucas walked home to the empty house.

Lucas understood that there was nothing wrong with the store or the owners; it was just that the times had changed. He eventually sold the building after refusing to set foot in it after finding his son. Lucas could not even walk past the store; the memories and the sadness were too much for him.

After Mark was buried beside Lucas' wife and daughter, Lucas returned home and never visited the cemetery again. He couldn't face seeing all of his family there. He existed alone in the old family house with only his memories.

Soon Lucas stopped eating. He spent long hours sitting in a rocking chair, refusing to turn on the lights at night. He quit attending church and refused to answer the front door when people came to visit. All he wanted was his family. The solitude was torture. No one and no activity could replace his beloved family.

A month later, Lucas was discovered in his bed, dead. The death certificate said "natural causes," but could it have been a heart attack or a broken heart that refused to beat any longer. We will never know for sure. But, now Lucas's family was finally all together again after so much tragedy.

Over the years, the building has housed several businesses; a flower shop, a gift shop, an antique store, a video/movie rental store, and finally a small restaurant. Currently the building stands empty – maybe.

Many of the people who have worked in this building have reported unusual sights and sounds.

People working there heard the sound of the basement door opening and gentle footsteps going down the steps, followed by a loud thud! When they rushed to look down the stairway nothing was found. All of the items stored in the basement were undisturbed. If someone walked down to check on the basement items they felt a wave of sadness come over them and many started to cry, not knowing why. If they touched the floor at the base of the steps, they felt a warm spot on the old cement floor.

There is a spot on the main wood floor that is always warm to the touch. When the sun light illuminates this warm part of the floor, people have reported seeing the figure of a woman lying down, not moving. She is dressed in the era of the 1930's. Employees of the store never walk in this spot or place any stock on this area. After they have seen this apparition, they feel it is disrespectful to violate this area because they are certain that it is Lucas' wife still on the floor.

For years after the general store closed, the backroom was the source of many interesting sounds and sights.

As soon as employees entered the storeroom they would complain of a feeling of sadness so strong that some had difficulty breathing. The air itself felt heavy.

If they stood still in the backroom and listened carefully, they heard the sound of a rope creaking against the rafter as it swung back and forth, back and forth. As long as the workers stood there the sound continued to groan, groan. If they stepped towards the sound, the groans would stop immediately.

In the corner of the backroom sits an old wood desk that has been there for years. No one sits at the desk more then once for they will find the chair warm, as if someone is already sitting there. Some people have felt a shove on their back as if being pushed from the chair. Occasionally, the sound of the chair moving has been heard when no one is near the desk.

Other times people have heard the sound of someone crying coming from the desk area. They've even seen small drops of moisture on the desk as if someone was crying so hard that their tears were splashing on the wood.

But most unusual is the feeling of happiness people feel when they visit Lucas and his family at the cemetery. After all this time and all the tragic events the family endured over the years; they are finally together.

Wild flowers spring up around Lucas' monument every year. Maybe he has found happiness again.

20.   The Green Eyes and the Shack

Every Ohio County seems to have a haunted woods and a haunted cemetery.   Miami County is no different.   Its haunted cemetery and woods are located next to each other on a lonely, seldom used road.

Back in the early 1900's, a husband and wife took orphaned children to live along with their own four children. This made for an interesting and busy household, but the couple seemed to enjoy this lifestyle. The children all loved this family and adjusted well. Some of the orphans only stayed until a family member could be located to care for them but a couple children lived with the family for years.

Jake and Mary Wilson and their family lived on a large farm complete with household animals and livestock. There were constantly a couple of dogs and house cats for the children to play with. Some of the kids became more attached to the pets than to the other children. And the pets were very willing to return the affection.

The farm consisted of pastures for the cows, large acreage for the crops, and a huge wooded area that was always left undisturbed. The family would often see deer wander out of the woods along with raccoons, skunks, and other critters. At times, though, screams were heard coming from the woods, but Jack told everyone that it was just a screech owl. All and all, it was very nice place to live and raise children.

One day while the entire family was away for the day the wood framed house burned to the ground. Nothing was salvageable. The only thing that remained was the basement. The cause of the fire was never discovered, but the husband guessed that it was due to the old electrical wiring. The family was in a state of shock and spent hours crying. After all of the pets were accounted for the children seemed to calm down.

The Wilson's all went into the barn later that evening to sit and think about their future. The parents knew that a plan was needed. At that time there were only the four children plus a couple of young orphans. Everyone had a different idea about what to do next; some wanted to move, some said to rebuild, and some said to live in the barn. The parents allowed each child to voice their opinion. They all talked until everyone came to an agreement.

The family had always dreamed of moving out west to Montana and decided that this was the perfect time for an adventure and a new beginning. Within a few weeks the livestock was sold along with the land and everyone squeezed into the car with their few belongs and headed west.

For a few years, the farm's new owner, Mr. Crawford, continued to farm the land. He left the woods stand because he felt that he had enough to care for without cutting down the trees for more farm land. Besides, he liked the woods and the wildlife that wandered near the trees.

Whenever Mr. Crawford drove his tractor near the old foundation of the house he felt a strange sensation come over him. Then one day he shut off the tractor and walked around where the house had stood. Then he saw it. A pair a green eyes looking at him. Not a person, just the green eyes. He turned quickly on his heels and raced back to his tractor. It took several minutes before his hands stopped shaking and his breathing slowed again.

While driving in the next field later that afternoon he decided that it was just the summer the heat causing him to see things. Not wanting to be ridiculed, he told no one what he'd seen. Really, who would believe seeing a pair of green eyes?

A few days later the same thing happened to him again. The green eyes were staring at him from where the house had once stood. That night at supper, he casually told his wife, Connie, about what he saw, trying hard to sound nonchalant. He was prepared for her to laugh at him or suggest that he was loosing his mind, but instead she said that she too had seen the green eyes. They talked for several minutes and agreed not to mention the eyes to anyone.

Later that year Crawford had the old basement filled in with dirt and used that location to park equipment. Many times he saw the green eyes looking at him; they were not sad or scary, just watchful. They never blinked.

After a few days, Crawford decided not to park any equipment on this space. He planted grass, shrubs, and a rose bush and kept it as their private park. The couple continued to see the green eyes, but now they looked happy.

Rita Arnold

Many of the surrounding farmers thought this was a nice remembrance of the previous family that had once lived there. Only the new owners knew exactly why they planted the garden setting.

After a few months of ownership, Mr. Crawford walked into the woods just to look around. He hoped to find some large downed branches or small fallen trees that he could chop up for firewood. The wooded area was about eight to ten acres in size but he was surprised to find nothing on the floor of the woods. He knew that none of the neighbors had been in there because there were no roads into the woods. A person had to drive through a field to get there.

Dusk was rapidly approaching and he knew that he had better return home. Then he saw it; an old syrup shack, the type shack built in the 1800's for making maple syrup. He knew there were plenty of sugar maples in the woods but he had no idea that anyone had made maple syrup in the recent past. This is a long, time-consuming process, and not many people in the area even knew how to collect the sap and boil it into the sweet syrup.

When he returned home, he told his wife about the maple syrup shack he had found and they both decided to walk to the woods together the next morning. His wife was excited about the find and eager to see the old syrup shack.

The next morning, right after breakfast, they both entered the woods and headed for the shack only to find nothing but an old foundation. The man removed his cap, scratched his head and said that he knew that he saw the entire shack the day before. In fact, he remembered seeing smoke rising from the roof as if someone was in the process of boiling the sap.

A few days later he was walking the woods and again saw the completed shack standing at dusk with smoke rising from the roof. No one was in sight. There was no evidence of anyone occupying the shack, just the smoke raising from the chimney.

This time he did not even tell his wife. He had some serious thinking to do. After several days had passed he remembered how happy the green eyes had looked after he created the park setting where the old house once stood.

That's when he knew what had to be done.

He soon drew up plans, bought some lumber and began to rebuild the old shack. He researched at the library for any details he was not sure about. His wife eagerly helped with the construction. As the project neared completion, they both noticed that the woods seemed to have a happier feeling. There was no longer a sad heaviness when they walked there.

The birds were singing louder. Even the wild flowers seemed to bloom brighter. The trees stood up taller and straighter.

A couple of times the couple felt as if someone was watching but never saw them. During the afternoon hours the couple thought they heard terrified screams coming from the shack they were constructing, but they knew they were alone.

A few days after the shack was completed, Mr. Crawford was walking past it and noticed the green eyes looking at him. They were smiling and for the first time they lowered as if a head were bowing.

The farmer whispered "You're welcome."

Weeks passed and the farmer went to the local historical society to look for any record of a disaster happening in the woods. After a few hours he found an old newspaper account of a tragic event.

Many years earlier a young couple had been homesteading on this property. To help supplement the farm's income, the couple collected the sap from the sugar maples, cooked it into syrup and sold it to the local general store.

Then, tragedy struck. The woman was working in the shack by herself while her husband was out gathering more firewood. They had just returned from their noon meal and she forgot to tie a rope around her skirt hem to keep it out of the fire.

While she was stirring the sap, her hem just grazed the blaze but it was enough to ignite her skirt. Her clothing burst into flames and her husband was helpless to save her. The shack burned quickly to the ground with the wife inside. For the rest of his days, the man lived with her blood curdling screams in his head and the guilt of being unable to save her.

After the sugar shack was completed, the green eyes were never seen again and the screams were silenced.

As the farmer read a description of the lady who burned to death, he finally understood. She had green eyes and red hair!

As for the Crawford's, they always left the woods alone, never again entering the rebuilt shack. He and his wife thought of it as sacred ground. The park setting over the old foundation became their quiet spot to relax.

Stubborn Spirits

21.   Money Matters

It's sad how money can change people and this has been true throughout the ages. Some people do great things with a new found fortune and while other people just go crazy; their personalities change and greed simply takes over.

In 1820, the three Wilson brothers decided to leave the crowded east coast and travel to the wilderness in Western Ohio. Here they could take advantage of the cheap land prices and set up their homesteads in a new territory. There would be new towns just beginning and they hoped to become important people. They were planning a great adventure.

Each brother wanted his own farm, but initially, they chose adjoining land so that it would be easy for them to help each other with the labor required. They dreamed of becoming important, rich, and prominent.

They left their wives and children behind in New York with plans to send for them when the men had found what they were calling the land of paradise and opportunity. After months of travel the brothers settled in what is now Warren County. They had driven their prized livestock with them for the beginning of a large, profitable herd.

Soon the Wilson's found the land that they dreamed of. It gently rolled to provide excellent drainage. A large creek flowing throughout the land with a variety of fish, and a great wooded area supplied plenty of game and herbs for food. The brothers knew that their wives would enjoy the wild flowers that grew in the woods.

The Wilson brothers decided not to send for their families until they each had cabins built for their families and shelters for the livestock. After they cut down the needed trees for the logs, the brothers began to build their cabins. While digging the ground for the cabins and planting gardens, the brothers noticed what wonderful soil they had found.

After many months of hard work the brothers were ready to bring their families to the new homesteads. It was agreed by all three brothers that two of them would go for the wives and children while Jonah, with the help of a couple of local hired hands, would tend to the farms.

Almost two years later, all three families were finally reunited in Ohio on the new homesteads. The farms were prospering and the brothers' hard work and long hours in the fields were starting to pay off. The families all seemed very happy with their farms and with each other, visiting every week. They were active in the local church with the children enjoying their school and new friends.

One day Jonah was digging a new foundation for the addition he planned to add to his cabin. His family of four would be increasing to five in about six months. While digging the foundation Jonah's shovel hit something solid, emitting an unusual sound. After a little work scraping away the dirt, Jonah was able to remove the square tin from the ground.

He sat in the shade of a nearby tree to examine the heavy box. What was inside took his breath away. After slamming the lid shut, he quickly and nervously looked around to see if anyone was watching. He peeked inside again and rapidly shut the lid a second time. He had to think. He needed a plan.

He placed the tin in his nearby wheelbarrow covering it with some tools and dirty rags and resumed his digging. Jonah became nervous, and continued to look around to make sure that no one was watching him. He needed to plan quickly. By continuing to work he was certain no one would suspect anything unusual. Jonah's brain began to race with several plans. Near the end of the afternoon he knew what he wanted to do.

When the time finally came to feed the livestock later that day, Jonah grabbed the wheelbarrow and headed to the barn. He carefully hid the tin in a wagon under some loose straw and went about his chores in the usual manner.

Much later that night after the children were asleep Jonah told his wife about his find: a tin full of gold coins, more than enough to make Jonah very wealthy. He was sure that she would agree to whatever he decided to do with his good fortune.

Jonah and his wife, Rachel, talked most of the night about what to do with the money. To his surprise, they ended the night with an argument and strong words. She wanted to share the new found wealth with the other brothers and the church. Jonah wanted to keep the entire find a secret and the money for himself. Jonah had no intention of sharing the money. It was his – ALL his and he saw no reason to share.

After Jonah fell asleep, his wife quietly slipped out to the barn, removed the money from the tin and hid it in the house under a loose board in the kitchen floor. She left the tin in the wagon as a decoy. She thought this would keep the money safe and they could discuss the situation more calmly after they both had some time to think things over. She didn't intend to deceive her husband; she just strongly opposed his selfish attitude.

The next morning Jonah was still angry with his wife and refused breakfast before heading out to work in the fields. Rachel knew that he was probably still angry but did not wish to continue the harsh words in front of the children. She never had time to tell Jonah about where she hid the money. She was sure that Jonah would become reasonable after some more time.

Later that day while Jonah was in the barn working, he looked in the wagon to check on the money. Discovering the tin empty Jonah went into an uncontrollable rage, yelling and stomping and running wildly about. Jonah headed for the house screaming that he had been robbed. He was sure that someone had stolen his new wealth.

His wife tried to tell him that she had hidden the money for safety but Jonah thought that she had done so for her own use. In fact, Jonah was afraid that she had already given some of the money away. Jonah's paranoia even convinced him that she planned to poison him. In his blind rage, he grabbed his rifle, shot his wife dead and then turned on his children, clubbing them to death. He stormed through the cabin, turning over the furniture and destroying anything he could grab.

When there was no one else to blame or beat he looked around the cabin wide-eyed in horror at what saw. Blinking his eyes several times and shaking his head, he gazed in stunned silence at the scene. As his breathing started to slow, he finally realized what he had done. Blood was splattered on the walls and large pools of it spread from beneath the dead, whose battered bodies were now unrecognizable. He slumped to the floor in a heap as his body shook violently and sobbed. What happened? Why? Could he really have done this horrible thing himself?

A few hours later, the truth was unavoidable. Jonah walked out to the barn in a daze, climbed up a stack of seed sacks, threw a strong rope over the rafter and jumped to his death. He had no reason to live.

The next day the bodies were found. A couple of days later the entire family was buried on a small rise near the creek under the shade of the trees. The two remaining brothers decided to burn down the cabin and divide the farm land. They could not bear to look at the cabin where this horrible tragedy had occurred.

After the ashes had cooled, the brothers filled in the area with dirt and let the weeds and grass grow wild. No one talked while this work was done. The brothers were grieving and worked in bewilderment with tears running down their faces.

The buried coins were never found, so the horror caused by what happened on that sad, sad day remained a mystery. As long as the farm remained in the Wilson family, no building was constructed on that location, whether out of respect for the deceased or because of the strange events that began to occur.

When working in the nearby fields, people soon started hearing screams coming from the site of the burned down cabin. The loud shrieking sounded as if someone was in terrible pain, but the screams would then suddenly stop. If anyone approached the site, nothing was heard but a heavy feeling of sadness came over them, so much so that some cried uncontrollably.

The barn stood for many years; first being used for livestock, and then, more recently, for storing equipment. To this day, people report hearing the creaking sound of a rope swinging from a rafter though no rope is found anywhere in the barn. No one lingers in that barn.

Others heard the sound of gun shots coming from that site. For years, visions of a man and woman arguing were reported by people driving past the place on the night of a full moon. Their arms waved about with their fingers pointing accusingly at each other. Then, suddenly, they both turned and faced the visitors, staring in surprise at being heard and vanishing within seconds.

Perhaps the strangest of all are the reports from people who walked over the ground where the cabin once stood and smelled the distinct metallic odor of blood. They searched the ground but all they found were grass and weeds. Most people quickly moved on and never returned.

There is still no record of buried coins being found. Perhaps Jonah is still guarding his treasure.

The ill had filled old hospital rooms,
And we find them all vacant now,
But hark! The ghosts and spirits say,
Some rooms will be filled they do vow!

The woods are always filled with trees,
Especially when they are near a park,
It's not unusual to see people running,
When they see ghosts floating in the dark.

Now you have read all of the stories,
We hope you've not been frightened,
The ghosts and their many doings,
Are signs of an interest heightened.

-Milton H. Arnold